Bridges of no Return

Nidel Koplin

Order this book online at www.trafford.com
or email orders@trafford.com

Most Trafford titles are also available at major online book retailers.

Printed in the United States of America.

ISBN: 978-1-4669-7159-2 (sc)
ISBN: 978-1-4669-7161-5 (hc)
ISBN: 978-1-4669-7160-8 (e)

Library of Congress Control Number: 2012923138

Trafford rev. 12/12/2012

North America & international
toll-free: 1 888 232 4444 (USA & Canada)
phone: 250 383 6864 • fax: 812 355 4082

I dedicate this book to my grandchildren
Sarah, Jacob, Mia, Charisse and Alex
Do not fear and follow the pursuit of your dreams.

My thanks to Sherry Jones and Tammy Stahl
who gave me support and encouragement.

Chapter 1

It was October in Colorado and snow had already shown its uncomfortable side, the one Karina Sheffield had not been able to get used to. The bitter cold accompanied by the crisp breezes chapped her skin with no mercy. She rubbed Vaseline on her dry skin day and night since regular moisturizers did not help her Latin skin used to humidity. The mile high city of Denver was not what she would have picked to live the rest of her life. She preferred a warm climate with a beach nearby where she could reminisce about her childhood and the country that she had so reluctantly left so many years ago. It really seemed an eternity now. Life had tricked her and she feared that God was laughing at her expectations.

Her friend Sylvia had offered her home to her in exchange of helping with the upkeep of the house and she gratefully accepted.

Sylvia Murphy had settled in Denver with her husband Jim. Karina had met her on her arrival to Colorado Springs, being the receptionist at the school where Karina was working. Sylvia was of German descent and spoke four languages making her a big asset to the diversified community that they worked for. They kept in touch with each other when Sylvia's husband was transferred to Denver.

Karina settled happily in the basement of the Murphy's very large home in July of that year and waited for the transfer to a school nearby, which wasn't easy since it was the best school in the area, to come through.

Karina moved to the living room and sat on the ten foot couch that her friend hated but of which her husband was very proud. She looked outside the picture window facing the beautiful weeping willows along the park—like street divide, swaying with the cold Autumn wind. Traffic moved slowly but steady. Karina loved to walk in the mornings but she liked to wait for the traffic to diminish once all workers had reached their job destinations. She had no desire to stay in Denver, It was a young people's city, beautiful and suited for all outside activities and sports. She had seen enough and was not interested in the sports available and whatever spectacular that was not seen by her would remain unknown. She was going to work and save her money to educate her children who were now ready for college. Also her scars from her divorce were too fresh to touch.

Karina was 5'6 with light brown hair and eyes. Her best asset was her mouth; full lips opened to show a perfect set of teeth that shined in an undulated smile which could be the pride of any photographer. Her full bust chest marked a very tiny waist followed by a nice round bottom held by the longest, shapely legs which were the envy of any woman. Karina Sheffield was of Spanish descent so she swayed as she walked as any good Spanish senorita has been taught to do. Her 115 pounds frame attracted the looks of both men and women. Now divorced, her kids grown and gone, she needed to work to accumulate a retirement package as she called it.

This whole experience may have come to teach her to be more aware and move with caution so she could gain some insight and find new tools to manifest the changes that were approaching in her life. She certainly could not afford a nervous breakdown. "Maybe later when I have enough money and more time," she told herself.

"I hope I have a job by the beginning of the year", she said to herself.

Her rationality fought to stay grounded and focused trying to tell her emotional self that everything always happens for the better, she put her head back and she drifted back to that fateful day when she left her homeland fearful but full of hope. Images of her life started to come in beautiful colors and shapes and tears started falling down her face. She missed her family and friends, her culture, and her language. She had chosen this life and she had to adjust to it; to the customs and beliefs and she was going to give it her best.

Born and raised in Isla Bonita, an island in the Caribbean Sea, of Spanish born parents, Karina had married a doctor, a surgeon, Enrique Bravo and had two children. They lived happily in Las Palmas, a seaport city in the Eastern side of the island. A focal point of the Spanish-American War. In 1898 the entire Spanish fleet was destroyed near its coast. Now, after believing they had paradise all to themselves, Marco Allende had started his fight against Miguel Juarez, the present dictator. No one expected what came about. Attacking an army garrison, Allende slowly and intelligently began the Revolution and the delightful fishing facility which Karina had loved so much, became the fearful fight for survival. Karina knew something had to be done to protect her family; trying to convince her husband was another story.

Luis Velez, Allende's best friend and confidante was captured and executed by Bolivian Army Rangers.

The efforts of the CIA to take him alive had failed and Karina started plans to leave Isla Bonita as she felt danger ahead. She had believed in Velez, he was her only hope, now she was not sure of what to expect.

In 1965, at the Plaza sitting in the middle of the capital, Allende made the announcement that beginning October 10, 1965, the port would be opened so that any citizen desiring to leave could do so but in so doing, they would forfeit any land or property they had in order to leave.

Doctors were paid $15.00 a month, working in poor facilities, poor or no equipment and lack of essential drugs. Her family could not possibly live a decent life under the poor circumstances now available to them and many like them. Thirty thousand citizens had fled the island and Allende started to make it very difficult for professionals to leave.

Karina had to go first with the children and then send for her husband, Enrique, agreed to this plan thinking that maybe they could save some of their property. She could get a Visa to Spain since her parents had been born there. This was a long process but the easiest, and later, work on a passport to the USA. It was not until 1969 that she could leave. Her children were six and seven, she was twenty seven years old and ready to start a new life in a different country; at least the language was no problem. She did not want her children to grow up in total disorder, it was sad but necessary. She was optimistic. On February 1969 she was ready to face her new world.

Enrique, a man in his thirty's was starting to look like sixty. His hair had started to recede and turning grey; he had developed a very wide waistline and his belt could not be seen because of his protruding stomach. Wrinkles were showing around his lifeless blue eyes and sadness and fear were written all over his very pale face. He hated to see his family go to a foreign country to search for a new life, he should be doing it, facing the inevitable he bid goodbye to his wife and children and hid the pain.

Karina shook her head trying to put the memories out, too sad to dwell on them. Enrique had become now just a shadow, she barely remembered him, but the desertion of her family and country was still very vivid in her mind.

Her goal was an American passport and citizenship and that she had obtained. Now she needed to make a new life for her children and herself and nothing was going to get in her way of doing it especially not another man. She had done it once and she could do it again; she made that promise to herself. She needed to put all those memories behind for now anyway.

Without another thought she moved to the kitchen to plan and start dinner.

Jim liked to eat exactly at 6:00 p.m. Sylvia should be home soon with all the extra ingredients since she still liked to shop every day like she was used to do in Germany.

Jim had developed Alzheimer and the disease was advancing rapidly. He loved to talk to Karina about the past and his time as a pilot but he would forget every other word or would repeat the same things over and over. He understood what was happening and he would apologize to Karina. Karina felt so sorry for him! He still enjoyed a good joke and Karina tried to humor him and since he would forget last minute's conversation, Karina could repeat her best jokes and he would laugh and laugh again and again.

"Are we about to eat, Karina? I am getting very hungry. The smell of whatever you are cooking is stirring hunger pains."

"Almost, Jim, waiting for Sylvia. I am making that stroganoff that you like so well. I am serving it with white rice this time instead of noodles. Is that alright? Still time to make some noodles . . . ."

Karina always tried to please Jim but he was easy to please.

"No, rice will be very good. Did you make any dessert?"

"Yes, I made pineapple upside down cake, but I don't know if you are allowed any."

"Oh, please cut a piece for me and hide it from Sylvia, please, please."

"I'll see what I can do."

The garage door opened announcing Sylvia's return. Karina proceeded to set the table.

Chapter 2

Karina moved her head back and forth as she recalled how it all happened and how daring and fearless the whole adventure was. Would she venture out into such an unknown now? Probably not, but it sure gave her confidence to fight for what needed to be done. Back in her bedroom she let the memories rush in and she drifted back to Spain.

Barcelona, Spain had gained economic strength and was welcoming people to come to the city and join the work force. It was experiencing cultural independence and was a lively Metropolis with bilingual signposts all over the city as well as newspapers and TV programs. The commercial side was very promising as it was mixed with a Mediterranean feeling. It should not be hard to find jobs.

Two other girls asked Karina to join her in her new quest and they offered to share expenses and help with the children. Karina could not have been more pleased. Ana Mendez and Melina Cortes hugged each other and kissed Karina. They proceeded to make the necessary plans.

Karina chuckled as she recalled that particular time. Everything was so new and they did not know what to expect. They were moving blindly but with certainty that it would be the first step toward entering the United States of America, the land of plenty.

There was no problem entering Spain and full of hope and relief, they rented a car. Karina was picked as driver while Ana was the co-pilot.

"It will be a while before we can visit places, we need jobs and money."

Melina interrupted her "The English, girls, the English, if we want to get to America."

Karina cruised North on the expressway, the direction Ana was giving her. It was mid-afternoon but it was cloudy and the sky looked like it was ready to dump a large amount of water. They passed a series of spectacular mansions "Not for us!" said Melina jokingly. "We want the heart, the center of labor and sweat which is our destination."

Traffic was heavy as people returned home from their jobs. Drivers were just like in Isla Bonita, everyone fending for themselves. Thanks to her experience, she could handle the traffic jam in front of her. Despite the tension, the three women were enjoying the beautiful architecture, the trees and lush vegetation.

With the help of Ana's knowledge of maps, they arrived at their apartment complex, The Gothic quarter near the Ramblas.

They parked in a very tight spot and proceeded to unload the car. The apartment was much more comfortable than expected: fully furnished, air conditioned with a small balcony facing La Sagrada Familia. The area was very convenient with many casual restaurants, bakeries, gas station; even a bank. The streets were well lit. The schools were close by and the school bus stopped almost in front of the old building bearing their new address.

The apartment exceeded their expectations other than the chipped cups and the plastic mats; they were delighted. The three bedrooms fit their needs, one master and two smaller ones. They flipped for the master. Whoever got it had to allow the others to use the tub. Karina was the lucky one and she took it as an omen of great things to come. The children occupied one and Ana and Melina the other.

The Catalan flair for beauty was well accepted all over Barcelona but they had no time to play, they needed to get busy and buy a phonograph and records to start learning English. They also needed jobs. They settled down and planned carefully their next moves. Karina wanted to take a shower and call her husband if possible. The kids were tired and hungry. Ana and Melina took them to one of the restaurants around the corner and their first taste of Spanish cuisine. It was well accepted by all especially the bread soaked in olive oil.

Next day, with eyes that spoke of their resilience to pain and hardship that they had experienced in their native island, their destiny started taking shape as they headed for Las Ramblas, the city's multi-faceted promenade going all the way through the old town and a magnet for tourists. Karina went to enroll the children in school and would meet Ana and Melina for lunch. Ana and Melina joined a class for tourist guidance. It was a two week preparation period and they would start working right after that.

Karina was excited at the progress made and so fast. She interviewed for a salesgirl position at one of the local museums dealing with local artifacts and because of her knowledge of the Catalan culture and love for history, she was accepted immediately. They decided to go celebrate and visit a local records store. Armed with a cheap phonograph and English language lessons, they headed for their new home.

There was no time for entertainment. They made it a point to save as much as possible, they needed to help their families and hopefully get Enrique out. Barcelona offered a lot of free activities of which they took advantage. The children were involved in school outings which they could attend and were enough for them. They were acquiring the English language with amazing speed since they were enrolled in a bi-lingual school. Karina was attending evening classes to finish her degree in teaching. Ana and Melina were both holding extra jobs at night. They spared some money once a month to enjoy a movie and they all looked forward to it.

Melina liked to sew, she even considered a designing course, and she put some nice outfits together for all as well as curtains, bedspreads and swags in the living room. She made the place really homey.

Things were working out and they had conquered the fear of being exposed to authorities or being picked up or even imprisoned. To them they were on the verge of total freedom.

They wanted to be solvent enough to see Spain. Madrid was first on their list followed by the Costa del Sol. Karina impressed on all that their goal was to get to the United States. To leave Spain they needed to master the English language and this required practice, so from that day on only English would be spoken in the household, except for the week-end. They all agreed as they went to their weekly Mc Donald's outing.

Life in Spain had become a routine but they made the most of it. They worked, they ate, they slept and so on. Once in a while each one would take time out to do some extra activity and they put all their money together to accomplish that. This way they could see some of the country or even visit the rest of Europe, of course in a real tight budget. Their time together was very enjoyable and they sang and laughed and sometime they even danced with each other keeping their ultimate goal in mind.

Karina made a point of calling Enrique as much as she was allowed which wasn't very much but he was reluctant to move, not yet. He still believed things would change and certainly get better, he always asked for time and patience. Sadly Karina accepted the fact that he was never going to leave.

Chapter 3

Three years passed very fast, Enrique had not been able to join them. The situation in Isla Bonita had gotten worst for him since he had been speaking against the government plus the fact that the government needed doctors, making it impossible for him to leave. Desperate to join his family, he started working on all kinds of illegal ways to find a way to get out taking his parents and other friends with him. This turned out to be very dangerous and was soon found out and put in jail. Karina tried to get him out through every means she knew about but it was to no avail, he died in jail within a couple of years. Karina did not take the news well and felt despondent for months.

Sadness had become weighty and dragged her around. At times it crushed her heart as if a snake had curled around her chest and she could not get rid of it. She had given her husband so many warnings and he kept thinking the obvious was not going to happen. She felt so impotent and the anger was eating her away. She booked herself in two more courses at the local university toward her teaching degree and enrolled the children in Summer camp. She forced herself to believe that life could be worse. Before she knew it, Summer was gone and Autumn was showing with night cool breezes. They took a couple of short trips to get to know Europe and kept working hard on their English and jobs. Their goal was not forborne.

"Karina, you have to go out and meet people. Concentrate on our plans to move to the U.S, but have some fun."

Ana Mendez was a short blonde, a little chubby but so full of optimism and zest for life. She was always ready for a new adventure or a good laugh. She was so grateful to be in Spain that nothing else mattered. She had become very fond of Karina and felt so sorry for her and the children. She apparently had met someone in England but said very little about the relationship; all the girls knew was that his name was Paul.

"You're right, I haven't seen Enrique for three years now and I can't remember his smile without mentioning his arms around me."

As she spoke, Karina had tears running down her face into her bosom.

"What about sex? You have been so damn faithful!"

"Sex was never that important in our relationship. We fell in love not lust. He was very religious and didn't want to use any contraceptives and after having Adriana and Nicolas, I was petrified of getting pregnant again so I was always tense and nervous and he respected my feelings."

The conversation woke up hunger pangs and they decided to go for empanadas. The evening ended with an all English conversation which they tried to do at least three times a week. They were determined to conquer this difficult language with all its exceptions to the rules and so many different pronunciations. They returned home singing and laughing.

"The telephone, Ana, someone with a very sexy, virile voice is asking for you."

Ana took the telephone to her room and talked for an hour. She returned to the living room with a very coquettish look on her face.

"Paul has invited me to a week-end in Paris. Would it be okay with you, is there anything special planned?'

"Tell us more about this guy. When are we meeting him? Invite him to come to Barcelona."

"Paul is carefree, intuitive and nurturing. He has brown hair, hazel eyes, and boasts an athletic shape. He works out every day and keeps a very healthy diet. He also deals with things in a very immediate way: he let whatever is bothering him out, get through with it and move on. He is much more spiritual than his brother Glenn. Paul is a lover of the outdoors and enjoys nature more than night life. He believes that if you let cares and problems fester inside, one can get sick and cancer can be one escape. Also, Paul has quietly explored the traditions of Buddhism. A positive thinker, he lives his life intending to be prosperous, happy, healthy and knowing that this will happen. I am totally enchanted with him and can listen to him for hours. I couldn't believe that he would like me but I have come to accept it and enjoy it. I want you to meet him and I will ask him on this trip."

"Does he have other family? Have you met any of them?"

"Yes, I met his brother Glenn but he was passing through on his way to a conference and didn't get a chance to get to know him well but from what I understand he's single and an insurance agent who owns his own company in Colorado USA. He represents the "noveau chic" and the inspiration of many a designer. His closet is filled with Lord and Taylor and some

Balenciagas. I would say he is sort of a narcissist but a very loving one. His style is exquisitely refined. He can name every wine by its origin and year. Autos are his preferred toys but always drives a Jaguar. Tall, blonde, slender, blue eyed, he leaves an aroma of Pierre Cardin as he walks by. He gives a feeling of assurance as he pulls his black Visa to pay the bill at one of the most elegant pubs in London. He tells me I am the most relaxing thing that he has ever met. I feel uncomfortable around him, I don't trust him. He drinks too much and is also a speeder, not mentioning his love for women. He had met a girl from the US and were staying at the same hotel. Paul did not know what was going on and had not met the lady. I did not see much of him."

"Sounds too good to be true. Be careful that your reach does not exceed your grasp, my dear." He could turn out to be a fantastic looking shoe but not your size. I'm sorry Ana, I don't want you to go through what I have gone through."

With that said, Karina kissed Ana on both cheeks and bid her good night.

The morning found Ana packing to go meet Paul. Karina and Melina joined her with a cup of coffee and kidded her about all the clothes she was taking, after all she was competing for Mr. Wonderful. Ana hit them with two pillows and laughed as only she could have done it. Little did they know that this was the last time they were going to see Ana as she left for Paris full of happy expectations.

Melina woke up to a telephone call at 6:00 A.M. It was Paul. He had not heard from Ana. She had decided to go for a walk before meeting him for dinner but she never came back. He had notified the police and was waiting for news from them.

Melina got up from bed and shook Karina from her deep sleep to figure out what they were going to do.
"Paul, at what time did she go for the walk?"

"I would say around 4:00 but, see, I wasn't home, I was at a meeting and came home, took a shower and waited for her, but no Ana. I decided to trace the route that I thought she might have taken but it got dark so I thought that maybe she was angry with me for going to work so I gave her time to cool off."

"But that's not like Ana. Ana is very easy-going and flexible."

"I know, that's one of the many qualities I like about her."

“I think that we better come to Paris and look into this.”

They hung up from Paul to answer a police call that left them numb. Ana had had a car accident, she was left on the side of the road; it was a hit and run, apparently. She had been in a comma with multiple lesions, and a broken arm. The police were trying to contact her friends and of course the man that she was meeting. She had awaken that morning but doesn’t remember anything personal, she has partial memory loss.

“We will be right there, as soon as possible.”

There was no sign of Ana at the hospital. All personnel was running amok exchanging notes and checking rooms looking for the patient in room 209 who had disappeared. No one could give an explanation because Ana was unable to move well. She had to have been taken or she took a wheel chair from the service room. All doors were ordered locked but Ana was nowhere to be found. The police wanted them to stay around until they found some kind of a lead.

Karina and Melina decided to take shifts so both could keep their jobs and take care of the children. Paul offered to take care of details and investigation which was a blessing because they did not know where they were going to get the necessary amount of money to find Ana. Karina felt a strong liking to this very handsome man. They decided to go to their hotel and put a plan together.

The police felt Ana was afraid of someone or something and that's why she had disappeared. They had found the word CAT written with lipstick on the mirror of her hospital room. Did she own a cat, does it stand for something, are they initials?

No to all. No connections. They will keep looking.

"There is no need for you to stay; Mr. Sheffield is taking care of everything. You will be notified and keep abreast of the events as they unfold."

"Maybe it is best that we make inquiries from Barcelona, we don't know anyone here."

Karina and Melina left after taking all the information necessary and Paul's promise of letting them know if he found anything, anything at all. They were both at a loss for any action and felt helpless and distraught. Ana was their family, they were a team.

Sadly, they kissed Paul goodbye and with tears streaming down their faces they looked at Paris with anger and fear as they boarded the taxi that was to take them to the airport.

They had visions of some events encountered in their native land that were appearing as a movie. They could not believe that their happy life had taken such a painful turn. They discussed the situation over and over but could not come up with any answers. They swore they would not stop until at least they found the body.

Chapter 4

Three months had passed and no signs of Ana. Paul asked Karina to come to London to finalize search and details concerning her disappearance. The police was closing the case but he was still hopeful. His brother would be visiting and maybe they all could put their heads together and come up with some answers. Karina accepted and proceeded to prepare for the trip.

Paul met her at the airport and drove carefully to his apartment.

"I set out a room for you in my apartment, no need to spend on a hotel; that way we will have more time together to discuss Ana. I hope it is OK with you".

"Sounds good. Thank you for all you have done. Wish someone sees the advertisement in the paper and connects with us." Karina sounded grateful, but somewhat hopeless.

His flat was a study of stylish flair with materials left in the natural state rather than painted or smoothed down. It faced north so it always had light and he had placed trees and plants all around as well. A water fountain placed on one wall gave it a feeling of sedation. The living room that served as den opened into a terraced garden; the two bedrooms facing it with glass doors leading to a wrought iron table and chairs that he used for dining. It couldn't have been more perfect. Karina settled down and met him in the terrace to start their plan of action. Tomorrow they will look around the city and meet Glen for lunch.

Their tour started in Piccadilly Circus Plaza, center of London. People from everywhere, dressed in everything imaginable walked passed them. They were to meet Glen at Clos Maggiore for lunch and tea. She was impressed with the Georgian house that actually opened into this French world.

"I'm going to like this!" she thought to herself.

Paul walked her to the bar where Glen was waiting. He was everything Ana had said about him plus she forgot to mention his charm. Karina's knees buckled under her and she thought she was going to faint. She had never felt this way before and she became really scared. She started to perspire and she excused herself to go to the ladies' room. Once there, Karina put a wet paper towel on her forehead and started breathing exercises until she regained her composure.

"This man is extremely dangerous, I better stay away from him", she said to herself and returned to the table.

Lunch was wonderful and very interesting. They all ordered sea bass with artichokes and leeks in a shellfish butter sauce culminating in peerless crème brulee. It seemed to Karina that Glen avoided talking about Ana but it could have been because he didn't know her very well. Paul was so involved with Ana's disappearance that he barely touched his food. It just did not make sense. Where could she be? They left for The Royal Academy of Art and the Burlington Arcade where Karina drooled over a gorgeous, blue, cashmere sweater that she couldn't afford.

Glen invited her to dinner and when she hesitated, he laughingly said, "I want to take you out, not asking you for marriage." They all laughed and she accepted.

"Not until we check with the police once more."

"Agreed" replied Paul.

Karina did not want to leave London without a visit to Harrods, it had been a dream of hers and she probably would not have the opportunity again.

"Is Kensington too far?' I'd like to see Harrods."

"Of course we can visit the world's famous store. I'll pick you up around five, go to Harrods and then The Serpentine where you will enjoy my favorite little pub."

Harrods was everything everyone said and after an hour of browsing around they left for the Serpentine and the perfect spot for a cozy date.

Dinner was an event of its own. Glen was so attentive and flattering that she could not help feeling floating around. It was great being alive again but also afraid of the turmoil of feelings. Karina was still full from lunch so she had lobster, scampi cocktail which left room for the specialty of the house dessert: Bread pudding. Glen suggested a walk around the lake which Karina happily accepted. They were losing the sense of time, they were so engrossed in their conversation. Karina's life in Isla Bonita, Glen's life in the United States, his departure from England, his mother's homeland. They both loved Europe but United States was their destination.

Karina asked for a rest, her feet were hurting and Glen stopped at a pub.

"I have the solution for that."

He found a bench where Karina sat. He went into the pub and came back with a bottle of champagne which he used to wash her feet. The effervescence and coldness did definitely the trick. They proceeded to end the evening early since she had a morning appointment with the police.

He kissed her goodnight and she knew she was not going to see him again, she could not respond for what could happen. She detached herself from his arms, thanked him and ran inside. Glen knew he was doomed to fall for good. She was perfect.

Karina returned to Barcelona knowing that Ana was not to be found and she, Karina Bravo, was about to cross a very dangerous bridge, a very unpredictable one. Glen called every night and wanted to come to Spain before he left for the United States. Karina fearfully asked him for the following week-end.

She could not recognize the feelings but it was like swinging in a hammock non stop and no one was pushing. It was a very disturbing realization that she was venturing out to reach this man that she barely knew. She expressed it to Glen in one of their conversations. Glen acknowledged that he was extremely attracted to her with the difference that he was enjoying it; asked her to relax and enjoy the moment. This was a new one for her.

Autumn turned into a season of loveliness because of its beauty and the feelings that she was experiencing. Every morning was a new picture of colors, temperatures, sounds that she had not known before. Melina teased her "My dear, you're in love".

Glen came to visit as agreed. Nicolas and Andrea had immediate rapport with this man so full of burning joy and optimism. Glen congratulated both on their perfect English and very polite ways. He discussed school with them and their plans for the future which included living in the US even though Spain had been a home to them.

"Who knows, maybe you will be visiting sooner than you think____and Nick, what is it like to live with all these women?"

"I kind of have become the man of the house with no rights"

They all laughed.

It rained all through the week-end but it did not stop Glen to rendezvous through the famous Ramblas. The rain put a spell on both of them and on the third night of his stay they stayed in a little hotel and made love. Karina was spell-bound, in thin air, something she had never felt. An energy, an electricity that warmed her all over as it relaxed her to the point of no return. She did not want these moments to end.

"You smell so wonderful!"

He whispered in her ear as he walked his fingers along her thighs.

"What do you wear?"

"Maja soap, it's made here in Spain."

She gasped as if she was going to lack oxygen very soon.

"We must keep lots of this soap around."

He touched her breasts and wiggled his index finger around her nipples. He kissed her on the lips and she responded with a passion that she found did not know where.

She sank into a gorge of nothingness as they consummated their passion. Total bliss wrapped both as they held each other tight as the thunder and lightning blew the window opened. Karina felt helpless and under a spell, one whose name was Glen Sheffield.

Karina did not know this kind of passion. She felt a volcano inside of her and needed to expel all that energy or she herself would explode, she wanted, needed more of the same. Glen felt her desire and warmth and it prompted him to make love to her again. They somehow shared a soul and traveled a bridge of no return as they climaxed together. The connection made traveled across time and space.

It was dark inside the room, the heavy rain had not stopped and had obscured the moon light. Karina felt quite safe in Glen's arms. She sighed with a moan of surrender. His arms wrapped around her protectively, she knew there was a new feeling perceived but she didn't know what it was.

"I think we should go through life doing just this."

Glen whispered in an out of breadth voice.

"What a good thought! No food, no sleeping, no work, just loving."

Karina was blissful, she turned away as his hands searched for her breasts, she rearranged herself to allow herself to kiss him over and over all over his face, neck, chest culminating in the most passionate of love making. Her heart had definitely unlocked itself to this man. She cried out in ecstasy and they both knew nothing could stop them now.

Reluctantly they got up to pack and get back to the apartment. Glen led her out the door and the feeling of starvation that she had felt was gone but she needed to be with this man now and forever. The thought scared her but the feeling was so wonderful that she saw it as worth jumping into it like Melina would have said.

They hardly spoke on the way back as Glen turned on her favorite music and held her tight every time he stopped for a light or a turn. Karina pressed his thigh in acceptance of his loving. Life was wonderful, she thought to herself, just could not get any better than this, no sir. They had to plan to talk to the children as soon as they arrived. She put her head on Glen's shoulder and dozed off.

Chapter 5

Melina loved Spain: the language, the culture, the food, the bull fights, the flamenco dancing and of course the sangria. She hoped to learn English to get a bi-lingual position in one of the embassies or government jobs. She was planning to stay. The men were courteous and generous to a fault.

She had been visiting Madrid and its surrounding towns as well as all the resorts she could afford on her salary. In one of her visits to Madrid, she met Carlos Acuna as she sat in an outdoor café sipping the very customary café con leche accompanied by the typical churros.

Melina was blue-eyed with undulating, shiny black hair cascading down her shoulders. She was 5'3, tiny, but very well proportioned. She liked to dress and dress well even though she had to follow a budget but shoes were her passion. This particular day she was wearing Grecian boots which she had traded with Karina.

"Nice boots. Italian?"

In front of her stood this tall dark man with chiseled features that made him appear Lebanese, speaking perfect Spanish. She considered ignoring him but he was too tempting and usually Spanish men did not try criminal behavior, at least not in public. After all one accomplished more, faster and easier by being charming and patient.

"Yes, as a matter of fact my friend bought them in Milano and I traded a pair of sandals for them. But they are getting really tight so I decided to take a break from my sight seeing and let my legs shrink again."

"May I join you? I would love to wait with you and maybe we can have supper later. Sounds good?"

"Sounds very good. Are you from this part of the country?"

Melina asked trying to keep a conversation going.

"No, I'm just looking around collecting information for my new book. I'm from Manresa, a little town near Barcelona, but I am hardly ever there.

I'm a nomad with a vicious love for Madrid. And you?"

"You are not going to believe it but I live in Barcelona although I was born and raised in Isla Bonita, but I don't want to go there now, maybe later, I want to enjoy the day."

"Ok, Let's not go there. What brought you here?"

"I also like the city and what it has to offer and also the coast is so romantic. Do you do any other kind of work besides writing?"

"I do not work as you so ardently put it. Not many have the luxury of working so little and still have a comfortable life style. In the last six years I have finished a book on the immigrants in Europe. It took me a while. Two of my other books were turned into movies—I love you, Charlie and She Misbehaved. They have been translated into English, maybe you have seen them."

"No, sorry I haven't, working and learning English take all my time. The little time I have, I tour Spain so I don't have time to go to the movies. What are you writing now?"

"I became very frustrated when I lost it. I couldn't go on; I didn't know how_________ all authors have to stop for a while to gain momentum."

He hesitated as he scratched his hair and continued in an apologizing kind of way.

"Sometimes I wish I had failed in my last book because it would have given me a challenge to search for success. I would not have been so demanding________ I am too passionate of my work. I write with a pen, on a notebook. I can feel more and better that way. I also can write anywhere, whenever the muse hits me. It's a lot of fun, one has total control of the characters, places, happenings. You can vent your frustrations without getting punished. One can even kill someone at the stroke of the pen."

"Did you ever loose any of your notebooks?" Melina inserted jokingly.

"Are you kidding? No, never. I hold on to them more than my own wallet. As soon as I get to port, as I call it, I get it all printed and put away. Why am I telling you all these?"

"Because you trust me? Because you had a terrible need to get it out of your system? Because you feel awkward around me?"

They both laughed.

"I feel very inspired to write about this meeting. What do you do?"

"I am a tourist guide but hope to move to America and become a nurse. There is one problem, I Love Spain and feel very comfortable here. So I guess I am confused."

"Maybe something can be worked out. Look it's almost seven. We have talked for hours. Let's go to my favorite restaurant and talk some more. Or maybe you want to just enjoy some tapas?"

"Tapas sound good."

The whole afternoon was divine and they decided to meet again. Before she left him, he handed her a couple of papers.

"Read this when you get home, maybe it will help you decide your future. I found it a long time ago in some magazine as I was trying to learn the language. I don't know who wrote it but I thank him because it changed my life."

Melina arrived in Barcelona with her head in the clouds. Carlos was the epitome of everything wanted in a man by any girl. She opened the pages handed to her and started laughing so loud that it called the attention of Karina and the children. Carlos was trying to talk her out of leaving Spain.

"Listen to this, you guys: "I found this in some magazine sometime ago and taught me not to expect to totally, ever, learn this language." It was a clipping taken from a magazine.

"If you've learned to speak fluent English, you must be a genius!. Read this. Reasons why the English language is so hard to learn:

1. The bandage was wound around the wound.
2. The soldier decided to desert his dessert in the desert.
3. Since there was no time like the present, he thought it was time to present the present.
4. The insurance was invalid for the invalid.
5. A seamstress and a sewer fell down into the sewer lines.
6. Upon seeing the tear in the painting I shed a tear.
7. I had to subject the subject to a series of tests.

English muffins were not invented in England nor French fries in France. Guinea pig is neither from Guinea nor is a pig. If the plural of tooth is teeth, why isn't he plural of booth beeth? In what other language do people recite at a play and play at a recital? Have noses that run and feet that smell. How can a slim chance and a fat chance be the same, while wise man and wise guy are opposites? You have to marvel at the unique lunacy of a language in which your house can burn up as it burns down, in which you fill in a form by filling it out, and in which, an alarm goes off by going on.

English was invented by people, not computers, and it reflects the creativity of the human race which is not a race at all. That is why, when the stars are out, they are visible, but when the lights are out, they are invisible."

They all laughed to their heart content.

"I am convinced, my dear Karina, that I should stay here in Spain. I have met the man of my dreams. How are you doing with Glen?"

"I think I am in love, all I can think about is the pleasure of his kisses, I have become addicted, I had never known what I feel now. It's just too good for tears and that article is true but we will get in an airplane and not on it and keep going. If you feel this is where you want to be, so be it. I hope Glen stays in my life even though those trips from America to here can be a decisive factor."

"Did you find out about his former life?"

"Yes, He met his wife in college. The only daughter of a very wealthy insurance magnate. They married and had two boys. They were married for twelve years in a touch and go relationship. She was unfaithful a couple of times. Of course, that's his side of the story, but I believe him. The father died and he stayed in front of the business. The divorce was nasty but you know in Insurance, you have clients and if you go, they go with you, so she decided to let him stay. I don't know the details but I'll keep asking. Apparently he is doing extremely well. He said if I go to America he will help me settle down in Colorado Springs where he has the business. Our lives are taking new turns, Melina I am just going with it. Adriana and Nicolas are going to start Middle School so it is a perfect time for a change.

Glen is going to send me literature on the school system and an application for a teaching job. I am excited for both of us. It's what I have been preparing for and with Ana gone and you staying, I feel the time has come. It is somewhat scary but exciting."

"Our lives have taken a big turn, haven't they? I hope some day we find out that Ana is alive and well and we can get together and look back to all the happenings as interesting but not important, just a new bridge to cross, one that seems fierce to say the least, a very unknown trajectory, but hopefully one that will lead us all to fulfillment."

"I feel sad that we have to separate but we knew from the beginning that this would happen. We just have to pray that Ana is found. I am happy for you and I will probably stay here, but we will keep in touch"

Melina was affirmative and committed.

"We can not distance ourselves, we have shared too much. I'll miss you."

Let's go out to dinner tonite, let's splurge a little."

They were both teary eyed.

"Sounds like a good idea. I'll meet you in the living room" agreed

Karina

They hugged each other one more time.

Chapter 6

Karina, the children and Melina had gathered in the living room to watch Carlos movie "She Misbehaved". It was announced that it would play once on TV and they did not want to miss it. They were all engrossed in the plot when the telephone rang. Nicolas, being bored with the girly movie, answered it. It was Daniela, Karina's sister. He yelled for his mom.

"Where are You?"

Asked Karina with her heart in her mouth. She was afraid for bad news.

"I'm in Miami. All is well. I did all that you suggested and little by little everything fell into place and here I am."

"Are you staying with your friend? Do you have money? Are you ok?"

Karina was always somewhat apprehensive when it came to Daniela. She always ended in the wrong side of the stick with everyone standing by poor Daniela. Karina was the liar, the problem, the inflexible one; the one who had to ask for forgiveness and forget until the next episode. But now it was different, we are talking about a new life. Once Daniela settled in, Karina would cut the strings.

"Yes, they have been wonderful. They have even bought me some clothes. I'm looking for a job but for the time being I am going to be a Nanny for a very wealthy couple—two kids."

"Sounds great. How are Mom and Dad, what are their plans?"

"They will never leave Isla Bonita. They do not want to bother with the language and culture. They don't think they can adjust. They have accepted life as it is."

"I understand. Right now the important thing is that you are out. I am planning to leave here very soon, moving to Colorado—Colorado Springs to be exact. I'll tell you about it later."

There was a long pause in the conversation as if both were trying to keep it going but didn't have much to say. Daniela broke the silence.

"How can anything seem so long ago and at the same time so yesterday? It feels like you and I were talking and fighting just the other day and yet I haven't seen you for so long."

"I know. Are you planning on staying in Florida? How's your English?"

"Pretty good. I start classes tomorrow though. I am going to give this move my all. I'll see how it goes but for now I'll stay here." There was a long pause as both waited for the other to say something. Karina felt some distance.

"Why don't I call you tomorrow and we can talk more. Glad to hear from you. Love you."

Daniela was an athlete, short, muscular, dark thick hair and always very tan because of her exposure to the tropical sun. She sported a very naïve manner that made people wonder where she was coming from. This was also her charm because everyone wanted to take care of her. She also had a temper, one that once she realized that she was not getting away with her whim, would explode like an atom bomb leaving everyone concerned fearful of her wrath and outcome.

Usually all around her kept quiet and speechless waiting for it to pass and it did until the next time.

No one contradicted her because of this and she made sure that it stayed that way by giving presents and little favors earning admiration for her good heart. She was definitely a study case. Daniela was always very jealous of quiet, studious, non athletic Karina. It was a feeling bigger than her, one that she could not control, because at the same time she longed to have Karina's attraction for people and even men. Karina tried to get close to her but Daniela was not a long term, steady person.

Karina still wanted to help her feeling protective and guilty. Their family had not being wealthy but Daniela definitely imagined being so and she believed it. Karina was glad she was save but trembled at what could happen next.

"You missed half the movie. It is pretty good."
Melina had a very proud look in her face.

"Tell me what has happened."
Karina asked with a pleading tone.

"Well a bad girl gets into a lot of trouble, just like girls do."

Nicolas interjected laughingly.

"It's a stupid movie. Nothing to brag about. You didn't miss anything."

Melina proceeded to explain the why of the theme.

"I like it and I am impressed. I have to call Carlos."

Melina left the room for her bedroom. Karina kissed the children good night and retired to hers. She had to think the new events out and figure what she was going to do. Her past was painful but forgetting it destines one to repeat it and she did not want to do that. She did not want to live in a labyrinth of half truths either. She did not want to condone Daniela's mishaps if Daniela was to grow spiritually but Karina knew deep in her heart that she was the only one to be able to get Daniela through this journey.

"I'll take care of this tomorrow" she said to herself emulating Scarlett O'hara. "I also have to start packing for Colorado Springs and a whole new life. Daniela is not going to spoil this one for me."

She put her head on the pillow and fell asleep immediately as images of Glenn danced in her head.

Chapter 7

"Colorado Springs had been called the national headquarters for 81 different religious organizations earning the nick-name The Evangelical Vatican and the Christian Mecca."

The guide started her tour speech with information that Karina had already looked up but it gave it a form of authenticity coming from her.

"America the Beautiful had been written referring to the views of this very attractive city. It's purple mountains majesty was definitely an understatement."

Where did Karina hear that phrase before? It was very familiar. She adjusted her earphones and continued listening.

Karina was impressed with the vistas and tried to ignore the religious implication. She wanted to like it since she had accepted a teaching position and had made her home here. The children were doing really well at school. They had adapted to the new environment and friends, they turned out to be very flexible to Karina's joy.

The Garden of the Gods was Nicolas favorite and Adriana had enjoyed The Royal Gorge and Cave of the Winds. Both were very impressed with NORAD (North American Aerospace Defense Command) "being built in Cheyenne Mountain placing it right next to Colorado Springs permanently securing the city's military presence. The Air Force Academy and its unique, famous chapel brought many tourists to the city."

Karina was interested in the history of the Ute Indian Nation whose descendants were still residing in the locality. Also of interest was the fact that due to being the most active lightning strike area in the United States, Nicolas Tesla chose it as the location to build his laboratory and study electricity. The guide certainly knew her history and answered all questions from the tourists with a smile on her face.

In their first tour they had lunch at the Broad moor Hotel and they were sold on their new choice of residence. As the tour guide described the different attractions, Karina couldn't help but think of Ana. She was a perfect guide and loved her job, what could have happened to her? Where was she? Karina still hoped that one day the telephone would ring and the melodious voice of Ana would come through with a warm hello and an explanation to her disappearance.

Nicolas voice brought her back to the present.

"Maybe I'll join the Air force" said Nicolas looking overwhelmed by it all.

"I'm going to be a lady of leisure getting massages at the Broad moor."

Adriana swirled on her feet and took a bow.

"Right now, my friends, you are going to study and get good grades. We need to get scholarships for college," replied Karina in a half-kidding tone.

Life could not be better, Karina felt she was close to reaching her goal. Glen was such help and so nurturing. For the first time in years she felt secure. She had a good job, the children were happy and healthy and she had Glen's love and support.

Steadily seeing each other for two years to date, Glen called to invite her on a weekend for the two of them in Estes Park.

"Get a sitter for a couple of days, you need time off and I need to have you all to myself."

"Sounds great. Let me see what I can do. The quietness and nature is exactly what this mind can use. Also sleep."

"Well, not that much sleep." It did not take long for Karina to accept the invitation. The children were very accommodating and she called Glen to let him know that she had made arrangements.

Glen picked her up early in the morning and drove almost silently to their destination. Neither wanted to break the enchantment surrounding their togetherness and closeness. Arriving at their assigned cabin, Glen fixed a couple of drinks and they sat looking at each other not wanting to lose the moment.

"I love you Karina. I want to marry you and take care of you and the children forever and ever."

Karina heard the words coming from far, far away. Even though she wanted to marry Glen, she didn't think he would give up his single life. She had even consider breaking up with him after this trip. She swallowed the rest of her drink.

"Are you sure you want to do this?"

"Yes, I do. I have tried to stay away but you are imbedded deep in my heart. I don't want to lose you. I am very happy by your side, I want to settle down."

Karina threw her arms around his shoulders giving him a big kiss.

"Yes, yes, yes."

In the flickering light of an almost burnt candle, they made love three, four times. They fell asleep in each other's arms. She woke up to the sound of bells, put her arms around him caressing his face with her mouth.

"Going to mass, querida?"

They both laughed and he proceeded to kiss her all over, gently, sweetly as she returned with a loving pat on his butt.

"I am going to fix something to eat."

"No. no I know a wonderful little bistro that makes the best Belgian waffles. Let's go eat there and then take a walk and talk about our future."

The future presented to Karina could not be more appealing. A house for all with a swimming pool, of course. Karina would have to work for a couple of years until he finished paying off his ex-wife. By then the children would be ready for college and he would take completely over.

"I have saved a little money for their education but it is not enough." This was a great concern for Karina.

"Don't worry, You will quit and I will see to it that they go to college. You just have to help now."

It sounded good to Karina and she accepted. It was almost dinner time by the time they got back to the cabin where they made more love. Karina had never realized what a wonderful sensation was received from the closeness of another human being. She was now totally addicted to his kisses and his touch.

This marked the beginning of wonderful nights together not to mention some days, if they could manage, of uninhibited love making. Cries of their fulfillment were shared as they both had ultimate release with total satisfaction.

The children could not be happier on hearing the news. They embraced both and started asking all kinds of questions.

"Where are we going to live? Do we have to change schools?

How fast is this happening?"

"Wow Wow-" exclaimed Glen. "One thing at a time. We have to start by finding a house. The wedding will be right after."

They found a great house in the outskirts of town and unbelievably enough close to Karina's school and the school that the children would attend. It wasn't even far from Glen's company. It also had a swimming pool but needed some work on the bathrooms and master bedroom. All in all the price was right and little by little it would be the perfect home as Glen proclaimed. Karina put up her savings and Glen matched them for the down payment. Life was perfect as far as Karina was concerned. They were married a month later.

Life continued to be the make believe love story so unknown to Karina where everything fell into place and ran smoothly as she kept the romance alive by believing that Glen was a messenger from Heaven. Some innuendos gave her room for thought but she quickly erased them from her mind.

Six years passed which saw the family grow and enjoy the amenities that an upper class environment offered. Karina was still working and Glen continued to be the perfect husband and lover. Karina was attending night school in her pursuit of a master in Education to be eligible for a coordinator job. Finally she was experiencing freedom without fear.

Studying late one night, the telephone rang and it was Daniela. Life had become too burdensome in Miami. Too many people, drugs, crime: she wanted to come to Colorado and start a new life.

"I have to talk to Glen first and I'll call you and make plans. Don't you worry, after all I'm your only family here."

"Please, please, get me out of here. I am now a legal secretary and good at it. I can find a job right away."

"You can apply from there if I send you information but first I have to talk to Glen and the children."

Everyone was in favor in helping Daniela and Karina proceeded to get applications to send her.

In less than a month, a very elegant Daniela showed up at the airport. She moved into the guest room and made herself at home. She had a week to find a car and report to work at a new law firm that was looking for a bi-lingual secretary.

Daniela of course, made all happen as she settled down as if she had belonged there all along. It seemed to Karina that Glen and Daniela knew each other from before because they were so attuned to each other. They certainly hit it off immediately since they were both athletes, something that Karina had never mastered.

Karina asked them about it but they both denied any connection. Was she facing a storm? Its winds and force had been felt inside her but all she could do was believe them. Karina hoped that Daniela was not a hole in Glen's past, Daniela had a way to manipulate and bring intrigue in her life. But maybe Karina was just obsessed with Daniela.

"Happy birthday sweetie." Daniela's voice brought her back to reality. "Glen and I have planned a night out so no cooking tonite."

Karina was happy although apprehensive about the surprise. Daniela always was on top of things. Why not Glen? She had to stop going there . . . "Gee, thanks I welcome a night out. Thanks."

The night went really well and exciting with great food and wine not to mention the ruby necklace and earrings that Glen gave her. Daniela gave her a family picture. It was a lovely time and Karina promised herself that she wouldn't question her sister and husband ever again.

They continued experiencing many happy times like these and Karina thought that Daniela had really changed and now truly trusted Glen's love.

Chapter 8

Daniela was enjoying her new life to the utmost. Her tennis game had improved tremendously since Glen was such an excellent player and had been willing to play with her almost every Saturday. They had become a great team and their lunches afterwards were the icing on the cake. Glen had suggested horse back riding on Sundays and of course this being Daniela's love and expertise, it sounded like music to her ears. Glen felt blessed since he had all he wanted at home and was able to exercise his athletic preferences with a very good partner at no expense to him, of any kind.

"Have you ever snow skied?"

"No. Not at all but would love to."

"We are going to have to visit the mountains: the best of Colorado. My favorite is Vail but you choose where you want to go. Aspen is the playground of the rich for winter sports."

"Does Karina ski?"

"Not, she is not the athletic type. She is better at indoor sports. She is an excellent Bridge player and mother."

They both laughed in agreement.

"When are we going?"

"Let's discuss it with the family and will take it from there."

Karina was happy for both and was glad that they got along so well. Many Saturdays, many Sundays and a couple of skiing trips to the mountains were enjoyed. Daniela could not ask for a better arrangement.

Another great afternoon had passed and Daniela took a shower and met with Karina in the kitchen. Many sacks of groceries were on top of the counter.

"Did you go shopping for groceries? What are we having for dinner? I'll make Tres leches cake (three kinds of milk), Ok?"

"Sure, Glen loves it."

"Karina, why do you have to work so hard and why do you pay all the bills? What is Glen's share? It seems to me he is doing real well and will continue to do well if he lives free of all obligations."

"We agreed to it until he pays off his wife and then he will take over. He bought the business from the wife, but will be through in three more years."

"Have you seen any legal papers?"

"No, I trust that he is honest and has my best interest at heart. I don't expect him to support my children, so I will continue to work until they graduate from college."

"This is not a first marriage, he has kids. You have kids, money with ex-wife, you have a little money saved, you work making good money. You have to be up front. At least share all expenses so that you would have some security when you retire. I bet you carry him in your insurance."

"Yes, I do, it's cheaper, he should know. Look I'm all right with things as they are. I don't want to make waves."

"Karina, I noticed that he pays for all purchases with a business credit card. All that belongs to the business, not you. Just open your eyes."

She picked up the dishes and moved to set the table.

"Idiot, I hope he takes you to the cleaners. Maybe I can get to enjoy it all."

It wasn't like Daniela to worry about anyone's misfortune. She was trying to get in Karina's good side and maybe set herself up for a more secure future living with her alone at Glen's expense and she knew all kinds of ways to do it, but Karina was not helping. Karina never saw anything her way, why now, she asked herself.

Daniela met with Glen in the living room who was starting a fire in the fireplace.

"How very, very cozy! One of the many things I like in the mountains. I love it!"

She got close to Glen and gave him a big hug accompanied by a kiss and Glen found himself responding. He did not know what he was feeling but he was shaken. Fear of being found out? The forbidden? Exciting? He threw caution to the winds.

He kissed her again and again.

"Where can I see you alone?"
"My bedroom at 10:00 tonight." Daniela answered coquettishly.

This started an affair. Glen did not realize the extent of Daniela's manipulation until it was too late.

They continued seeing each other after their tennis games and horse back riding. Karina did not have a clue. She trusted both. Glen continued living a fantasy of deception and lust and disconnected himself from the genuine, actual life that he had with Karina, of the people that truly loved him. Like an addict he tried to get through an hour, a day, another shared family experience. 'Fidelity is not to the person one is married to but to the devotion and memories shared,' he told himself, and he was not giving his family up. He felt like a galloping horse racing out of its gate and he could not stop it, for now anyway. He did not plan this, it happened, not ever thinking that Daniela played a big part on it.

"My dear, I need to be with you, I ache for your arms, your kisses and your body. Let's meet at the house at about 1:30. Karina will be in school and so would the kids."

Daniela sounded desperate.

"You are a real devil," responded Glen. "I'll see you there."

They did not waste anytime getting undressed and making love when suddenly the door opened and the figure of a woman was suddenly in front of them.

Karina had felt bad with a terrible headache and decided to take the afternoon off. She could not believe what she was witnessing. She assumed that they could not deny something so obvious, so painful, so agonizing.

"Get out of my house, right now."

She managed to utter and in a very low almost in a whisper she addressed her husband: "How could you?"

"Please leave the house also right now!"

She moved to the kitchen as they both started to move out. Glen came to plead forgiveness but she would not even let him in the kitchen and locked herself in.

She wondered if she would be able to breathe again.

Karina had thought that Glen's love would keep them together forever. Now her impression of her life with him had been shadowed by a web of lies, as well as thrills, inexplicable episodes and the fear that she was losing all.

The whole picture of the two of them seemed to be swallowing her life. Her emotions were going through mountain highs and lowest of lows. She had never known such despair.

Again she had to think of the children and she said to herself:

“Ah, love is a commodity of the middle class, you are above this. Survival is in your blood.”

She buried herself in her job as she was being offered the coordinatorship that she had been working for. This meant more money and possibly less work so she could easily manage her life alone.

After the divorce she found out that Glen’s wife was still co owner of the company, his kids were to inherit everything he owned and the purchases made for the house belonged to the company and his wife readily sent for them. She felt very betrayed by the man she had trusted blindly.

Daniela had moved out of Colorado Springs, possibly to California and Glen was still president of the Insurance Company, but controlled by the ex- wife.

Adriana and Nicolas were holding up very well and very supportive of their mother. Both had found good jobs while awaiting acceptance in the colleges they had applied and hoping for scholarships.

By September, Karina heard the good news that both kids had settled in their respective schools of learning and would start pursuing the careers of their choice. Karina would help with the tuition and board but they had to take care of the other expenses like food, clothing, entertainment, and books. Both Adriana and Nicolas were very thankful of the big help and let their mother know it.

Karina had saved enough money and with her teaching salary, she could manage to help them. Again entertainment was taking a second, if not last place, in her life. She had to do this for them and she was not apprehensive and held no regrets. She was facing a new bridge to cross and she looked forward to what was ahead. The next four years promised to be very demanding but promising. She had to plan and budget her life once again except this time she had more know how. At least she would have no time to feel the heartache and anguish that the break-up of her marriage had left. She was thankful for the job she had which gave her security, something she did not have when she started this journey.

Chapter 9

There is a seemingly endless selection of options to spruce up one's landscape whether one chooses to stay alone or find another partner. Karina was grieving more than she ever did when she lost Enrique since this relationship had been more intimate, closer, a passionate friendship. She swore that she would not get involved in another relationship. Before starting her new life she had to stop and look at her landscape.

"Because a husband has disappeared, one can't stop living, but face what worked or didn't and there is no better time to evaluate one's likes and dislikes and what needs to be changed, than at this time" she told herself.

She also looked into what she had to offer and then sketched a new plan of action. Some things had to be removed completely, number one: her need to help

Daniela, she was nothing but a snake in her garden. Karina realized there were some things that needed to be introduced in her life. The family is karmic and part of her past. It had to be put on hold although not forgotten, she didn't want to repeat the same mistakes. She was now an American citizen and she had grown by leaps and bounds as she established roots for her children. Now she needed to give them wings with a strong support system, to be a catalyst in their lives without getting involved.

Life for Adriana had been up hill till now, kind of a Cinderella story. Since her teen years she gave signs of her ability for business.

"Mom," she would say, "Can I have what you are not saving from the Xmas decorations?"

"I am selling them to people to be used next year." She sold them to the neighbors and friends.

She used all her efforts and perseverance to get good grades and she took business administration, computer science and accounting at the junior college. This opened the doors to a high paying job in a well known financial company. She worked hard and became sales manager. Five years later the company was about to declare itself in bankruptcy, Adriana took over and pulled it out. She merged with a cosmetic firm whose products have been very well accepted all over the world.

She grew up into a beautiful woman, very serene with the sweetest voice, like a pool of water.

Nicolas wanted to be an engineer, always did. He received a scholarship and studied non stop until he got his degree. Now working for a big firm, he is manager of production and loves his work. When his mother asked him how he liked his job he answered "Imagine going to have fun everyday and getting pay for it!"

Karina couldn't complain. On the drive home the houses around her seemed like mirages and the people nothing but shadows but she is pleased with her job as a mother. It's the romantic side that she hasn't done well. Every two weeks at least she sees Glen in her dreams and at some point in the dream he leans across and whispers "I'm so sorry. I have been a coward," and she wakes with her heart booming and for a few moments her life throbs with possibilities. She touches the hot water bottles with which she had replaced Glen, turns over and sobs herself to sleep.

Five years have passed. Karina feels the need to move away from Colorado Springs, away from all the memories. She started checking on retirement communities around the United States. She had settled for Magnolia Meadows in the South. The gated community was created in friendship with the wonders of nature. The houses were built among pines and oaks giving a lot of privacy. Private lakes and walking trails offered security, peace and tranquility. It actually offered all the amenities that anyone would like to enjoy.

Karina sensed a lot of energy coming in a familiar wave of expectancy as well as joy. She needed to work five more years to secure more income for her retirement, "renewment," she called it. She wanted to renew herself not tire again. Whenever she felt anxious she listened to soothing music and breathed deeply. This was her tranquility moment. She needed to learn to trust again. The problem is that it isn't that one can not trust people but that she can not pick the one to trust. Life throws you the experience and one has to deal with it. She didn't believe in drugs to feel well and had brought up her kids thinking this way. She was lost in thought when the telephone rang. It was Andrea.

"Hi, sweetheart, are you coming for Thanksgiving? Nick will be here, you know."

"Yes, Mom, I need to discuss with you guys my search for fulfillment. I have met someone and I'm having a lot of struggle, conflict with it."

"Oh my bebe, We need to meet the lucky guy and yes, we will discuss it but you don't have to seek fulfillment by established routes, you know that.

I have some plans to tell you about also. I am really looking forward to being together again. See you then. Love you!"

Thanksgiving had become their most looking forward—to day or weekend. They were able to discuss all their plans and problems and help each other to solve them.

After a succulent dinner of Turkey and all the trimmings, they sat down to reminisce and discuss what was going on in their lives.

"I love what I am doing and with the new sex revolution and women finding themselves, I intend to stay single for a long time."

Nick started the discussion.

"I am going to take the Silva Mind Control classes and also Transcendental meditation. It's about time I start learning more about what you, Mom, preached all our lives. I see a girl that is very much into all this higher and more perfect order. I am certainly turning inward. I also started jogging. That's my experience right now. Your turn little sister."

"Yeah this is also a decade of murder, kidnappings, bombings and hijackings, my dear. Women are in and becoming free and the racial issue culminated in the book Roots by Alex Haley. We have started to leave the Me syndrome for The We. I am confused. I want to get married and have a family but I also want to continue with my business."

"But dear, if you discipline and organize yourself you can do both. That's the beauty of it all. What does your boyfriend think of all this?"

"Oh he's all about my continuing with my job but also manage the house and take care of the children. I say he has to come half way!"

Adrianne waves her hand to show her disapproval.

"I see problems ahead" started to say Nick, when Adrianne stopped him with

"Don't take his side and show your Spanish machismo. This is America."

"No honey, you can not start a relationship with demands. You catch more flies with honey, it's the Spanish way also. You have to make him believe that he is in charge at all times while you get away with murder. It's easier and he can save face without hurting anyone."

Karina still believed that women had to protect themselves by being manipulative. It worked for her mother and for herself also. If Daniela had not gotten in the way, she would still be married to Glen.

"Tell us about this man you feel so strongly about."

"His name is Christopher Fuller. He's a doctor, a gynecologist. He's not too tall, brown hair and eyes with the greatest sense of humor. He is finishing his residency and has being offered a position in a very good hospital in Los Angeles. He wants to take me with him. That means I have to leave my business."

"Can't you sell it? Keep part of it, something like that, maybe get someone to work it for a profit until you settle in Los Angeles".

Karina was not too sure of what she was suggesting.

"We certainly have to work it out to each other's advantage. We still have almost a year to work on it."
Adriana sounded calmer.

"Oh well that should be long enough. When do we meet him?"

"He wanted to come now but his hours are terrible. He says things will get better after he starts to work regularly. What about you Mom?"

"Well, I decided to sell the townhouse and move to Denver. I am applying for a job there. I need to work about five more years and then move to this retirement community that I find charming. I want you kids to come with me to see it and tell me what you think."

"I am glad you decided to leave the Springs. That jerk is still around and also the memories," interjected Nick. "Denver is beautiful. The mile-high city, wow."

"Don't you have a friend there, a very old friend?" Asked Adrianne with concern in her voice.

"Yes, I do, I intend to get in touch and maybe I can rent a room from her until I get organized."

Sylvia had been the first friendly person she met when she started teaching in Colorado Springs. She was a traveling nurse who spoke four or five languages and German by birth. She "needed" to meet a rich husband that would support her and the traveling helped her do just that. She met the father of a child she was taking care of, married him and had moved to Denver where his business was. She apparently had met her goal. Karina kept in touch with her and visited her a couple of times. They had become good friends.

"More Pumpkin pie anyone?"

"Yeah, yeah"

Adriana and Nicolas danced into the kitchen.

They moved to the den with their plates full of pie and ice cream. It was another great Thanksgiving get together.

Karina smiled as she recalled the celebration. She missed her kids.

Thinking about the ice cream brought Karina back with a yearn for the mountain of calories. Sylvia walked in at that moment and joined her in satisfying the need for the much appetizing food.

"Are you still considering the Meadows for retirement?"

Sylvia was always apprehensive when talking about her leaving.

"Yes, very much so. It has all that I need and fits my budget.

"Have you put a time limit on your move?"

"Yes and no. I need to make more money and it will take a while to build once I decide on it."

"Then we will be enjoying you for a while longer"
"I am afraid so."

They moved to the den to finish the ice cream and watch a movie.

"Were you reminiscing about your early days and the Kids? Do you still think about Glen?"
"Yes, to both, now I need to think work, Money and The Meadows. I will not find myself in this situation again."

"Don't make promises to yourself like that, you are too hurt. Who would have thought that your own sister would have played around with your husband? You have to trust your family, isn't that what the church teaches or society, I don't know, but don't blame yourself. You are fifty five years old and look like thirty; it's Glen's loss. Let's have some brandy before bed and look forward to tomorrow."
Sylvia put her arms around Karina's waist to show her support and went for the brandy.

Chapter 10

Karina felt as if she had been guided to where she could find the right place to be and contemplate with no disturbances. There was a magical energy that lifted her spirit to be aware of her soul and purpose in life.

"La dolce vita is not A LUXURY DESTINATION BUT A STATE OF MIND," she told herself. Magnolia Meadows did not look like anywhere else, simple, country-like and far away from the nearest city. She was delighted with her choice.

Some retirees travel to Magnolia Meadows for its breathtaking views of the Ozark mountains and the crystal availability not to mention the healing waters. Others just to be pampered at the many spas. It appeals to a generation that wants to come to terms with the past and bring the outcome into present time.

Karina loved the porches incorporated in the homes blending with the climate humidity reminding her of her Caribbean background. This mixture of European classicism and tropical touch gave her a feeling of belonging. Images of her and her family sitting on a hot summer evening, some swinging in the proverbial hammock, comforted her. She had idealistic dreams about being very happy here. With stars in her eyes she treasured the thoughts about her life in the paradise she had found.

Her house had not sold and she needed to accumulate social security benefits to supplement her income.

"You know you can stay here as long as you need to. Jim loves you and thinks you are a great help to us."

Nervously spoke Sylvia.

Karina was a great solace to her and helped her keep her marriage together.

The ring of the telephone gashed their thoughts and Sylvia quickly answered.

"We want to talk to Karina Bravo. Is she still available for a position?"

"Karina it's for you" and handed her the telephone.

"We have a position teaching ESL (English as a Second Language) starting in February. We would like for you to come for an interview."

Karina almost jumped with joy and promptly made an appointment for next day. She embraced Sylvia and swung her in the air.

"I'm in, I'm in" she cried out.

The school was half an hour away from her and big and beautiful. The ESL program was growing rapidly consisting now of three regular teachers and six who taught one or two classes. Karina was to teach full time mainly English. She excitedly accepted the offer and stopped in a supply store on the way home to prepare for her new experience.

February arrived very cold with snow coming down as if there was not going to be an ending to the season. Karina slipped and slid all the way to school. It was a good choice to leave earlier than necessary to avoid stress. She arrived on time to a classroom full of anxious faces. The children were mostly Mexican and polite and eager to learn. Karina was delighted. With no discipline problems, her teaching moved quickly and successfully.

The year went by smoothly with no big problems and plenty of rewards. The parents were so grateful for all the support Karina was giving them, they brought food and offered all the help Karina needed. The principal was in awe at how much she had accomplished in such little time.

At home Karina faced her friend's problems. Jim's Alzheimer was advancing fast; too fast for Sylvia to handle. He was behaving very odd while expressing anger and animosity toward Sylvia. Sylvia was not the strong person that she appeared to be and started depending on Karina for help dealing with him. Karina had to spend many hours just consoling her friend who cried incessantly. Jim was oblivious to all of it but counted on Karina for talking mostly nonsense and a lot of stories about his past. He still enjoyed her jokes making a little easier to bear.

Karina started to spend time at Cherry Creek Shopping District enjoying the tree-lined streets with their cafes, spas and galleries as well as the beautiful fountains. She spent endless hours at the Shattered Cover Book store reading. Other times she visited the 16th Street Pedestrian Mall with its grey and pink granite pathway lined with trees and flowers, very relaxing. Latimer Square was another get away for her meeting Sylvia for lunch once in a while. There was not really any social life for her. Men were either too young or too backward, not worth her allowing time that she needed for her work both at school and at home.

"Karina, there is a gentleman who met you at our last party who wants to take you out."

Sylvia had a very tantalizing voice.

"Why don't you try it?"

"Sylvia, my dear, is that the political refugee gentleman? I'd like to go dancing with him but that is all. I am not interested in a relationship."

"Yes, he is, he is most interesting and very charming. Jorge Vera from Chile."

"Of course, he was a diplomat, he knows how to charm but what else can he offer?" Does he have a job or is he still on Government Aid?"

"That's for you to find out. We are invited to a wedding reception, why don't you be his date?"

"Why don't I meet him there? That way I'm not obligated to be with him all the time if it turns out badly."

"Ok. I'll arrange it somehow. What are we going to do with Jim?"

"Let's get a sitter. He won't even notice."

"Sounds like a plan" returned Sylvia with a mischievous look in her eyes as if she was getting away with something.

For five years Karina had nursed her wounds, filed away the divorce papers where she didn't have to look at them ever again, and lived the live of an independent woman. She didn't love her independence that much and if that was there for her, she could be tempted. She would give him a chance and she leaned back on the recliner.

Lately she had been feeling restless, worried that the rest of her life would be lonely. Do a few projects around the house, go to work, watch television, get up and go to work. Something had to change but she didn't know how to proceed.

"You seem lost in thought, not like you. What's up?" Sylvia's German accent startled her.

"I miss the friendship and camaraderie of a lover to come home to, someone I could wrap my arms and in turn he cared deeply for me. Sometimes I feel very tired. I need comforting but it became too complicated to meet someone normal. I compared everyone to Glenn and guess I didn't want to find out that Glenn's arms and love were unique. It makes me nervous just thinking about it." Karina was kind of excusing herself.

"Have to jump in the water, my dear. You will swim again."

Karina smiled, checked her teeth in the big mirror in front of her.

"We'll see."

She looked very good in her new little black dress. It was going to a lot of engagements because she could not afford another one. She added her string of pearls and earrings and a wrap that Sylvia lent her. Laughing out loud, they left for the party.

They were not there very long when a man's voice, very softly murmured:

"Can I get you a drink, gorgeous?"

Karina turned to face a tall, well-dressed, grey-haired man showing the whitest teeth she had ever seen in her life.

"We met at the Reeds. Remember?"

"Yes, I do and you can get me some soda. Thanks."

They started talking telling each other about their mutual backgrounds. Soft jazzy music came from the front of the room.

"Dance?"

The evening went on without too much apprehension. They were both at ease with each other and all in all it turned out to be a very pleasant evening with a lot of dancing which they both enjoyed.

Karina's mind started to work overtime. 'So now what, this has created an unnecessary problem.' She thought to herself as she took a couple of breaths.

"Hey, you looked good together and you were so great on the dance floor. We stood up just to look at you whirling around. Are you going to see him again?"

"I don't know it's too scary. I'll just take it easy."

But she forgot about the caution her intuition was giving her and went for it.

They started seeing each other and on and off they kept the friendship going as she called it. The movies, the dinners, the visits with friends were all great. It was the alone time together that was not gelling. Karina could not handle the intimacy. She felt very uncomfortable without a commitment.

The relationship started to wane and their time together seemed stiff and awkward as if they didn't know what to do with each other. A big silence filled their time together and Karina knew it was over . . . And knew it was her fault; she was not willing to try.

"We need to talk."

She approached Jorge one evening after work.

"I am not ready for an intimate relationship, I can't handle it and it isn't fair to you not to be able to get closer and have one. You are a wonderful man maybe a couple of years from now, if you are still single, which I doubt, we can try again. All I can offer now is a real true friendship."

Jorge did not want to stay for more. He leapt out of his chair and rushed out of the house ending the relationship.

Karina did not want to go through something like this again and she swore men off. She was going to concentrate on her move to Magnolia Meadows and enjoying her grandchildren.

Karina longed for an escape, one that would allow her to put her thoughts together without input from anyone. Now was the time for a long drive in a convertible where she could feel the cool air and play her favorite music with no reservations. This should clear her head so she could plan.

Without any other consideration, she asked for time out at school and took off without a destination, she would drive until she could stop and come back when she was ready. It sounded crazy but she needed to do something crazy.

Karina started out at six thirty in the morning. She was totally relaxed and stopped for breakfast. After, she took a brisk walk around the parking lot to calm whatever nerves were still frazzled. She had planned for a late breakfast and an early dinner so as to enjoy the landscape as much as possible.

Her first day was quiet, so much so that she could hear the silence. All was so peaceful and her head started to clear up when she stopped for dinner at her small hotel. After taking a hot bath, she was not thinking anymore, her brain went into neutral and she went to sleep without a care in the world.

The sun coming through the window shades woke her up, and she promptly got up to continue her adventure. She had a glass of juice and a piece of toast and coffee to go. She drove all the way non-stop into a little town that was having a parade. Karina loved parades and their music, so she stopped to watch. How very wholesome it looked!

Happy as a lark, she continued on to wherever the road was taking her. A small park with a lake reminded her of her hometown, she found a bed and breakfast and decided to spend the night here. She rented a kayak and rowed down to the other side of the park. Someone asked her if she wanted to be taken back or was she going to row back herself.

"Pretty tiring to do both ways. I suggest you go back with me. Very relaxing little trip. I gather you are not from these whereabouts."

No, I am passing through and yes, please take me back."

Karina stayed here for the rest of her trip and returned to Denver a new woman ready to face her life ahead.

Chapter 11

"Mrs. Bravo, your house will be started next month and we need for you to visit and choose the different aspects, fixtures that you want in your new home. When will you be able to stay with us for at least a week-end? We will provide lodging for you."

Karina was surprised, happy, excited and very scared. She was not ready to make the move yet. When her house sold, she had traveled to Magnolia Meadows and contracted to build on a chosen lot. She gave the lot she had purchased eight years before as down payment and returned to Denver. She had figured ten more years, but here it was: life was happening again while she was making other plans. She had no choice than to proceed.

"I'll figure out when I can come over and will call you. I have to get vacation time and get my financial affairs in order."

"All you need is $10,000.00 down for us to start the proceedings and we will talk about the method you prefer to pay the rest after you decide on what you want."

"That sounds good. I will call. Thanks."

How she wished she had someone to guide her or be with her for support!

She consoled herself by remembering the words of a teacher she had. 'Your sense of direction may be off but your intuition can steer you. Just choose your focus. If you feel there are too many mixed messages, set boundaries, realize your limits and go slow.'

Her focus was this move that was moving faster than a speeding bullet as far as she was concerned. Sylvia approached her and putting her arms about her offered her a loan that she could pay back when she could, at her leisure. This was a way to thank her for all Karina had done for them. This would certainly help; so Karina accepted with tears in her eyes.

Karina started to plan her trip to her new home.

There were plenty of rough spots in the months to follow especially when figuring out the money situation. She struggled through extra jobs to accumulate more cash and many times she wept in self-pity. This was not the Karina who left her country full of hope for a better life so every time she found herself approaching another melodrama, she nudged it into a positive direction and pulled her self-esteem back up again. She started looking at the prospect of packing and cleaning her belongings and even looking at fixtures and furniture for her new abode.

"Sylvia, will you go to Magnolia Meadows with me? It will not be a fun, nor a restful vacation but I could use the support."

"Sure, sounds like fun and I'd want to see this place you talk so much about. Just let me know when so I can plan ahead. I have to get someone to look after Jim."

"In two weeks my dear. Is that plenty of time?"

"I can manage that." Sylvia was excited about going with Karina and getting time away from Jim.

Karina started looking at the prospect of packing and cleaning her belongings. Thank goodness she had sold all her furniture with the house and most of her household treasures were given to the children. She went to the basement where she kept her life belongings and started sorting out the different boxes. One box was totally unfamiliar and in looking closer she noticed the name Daniela written on it. She nervously pulled it out and was deadly surprised to find insurance papers in it. She was unaware that her sister dealt with insurance. Different folders bore different names that she did not recognize except one that gave her goose bumps . . . . Ana Mendez.

"What in the world!?"

Karina was really puzzled and opened the folder finding to her surprise an insurance written on behalf of Ana with Paul as beneficiary. $5,000000.00

She held the folder close to her heart and wept until her eyes hurt.

'Impossible, I must call Melina.'

Melina answered the telephoned totally out of breath.

"Karina, what a treat to hear from you. How are you?"

"I don't know how I am. You have to help me sort it out. How are you and the family?"

"The kids are driving me crazy but Carlos is a dear. He's researching a new book and left for Germany and when he is not here these two angels take advantage but we are healthy and happy. Tell me, what's up?"

"I found an insurance written to Ana Mendez with Paul as beneficiary. Melina, It's for five million dollars. I don't know if it has been collected or if Ana was killed because of it and why is it in Daniela's possession?"

"Oh WOW! What are you going to do?"

"I don't know, that's why am calling you. Maybe we can figure something out. I feel like Don Quixote fighting wind-mills. What if Glenn had something to do with it? I could be involved!"

"Don't jump to conclusions. Let's call Paul for a starter. Don't you think? And also if it were that important why did Daniela left it behind?"

"I don't know, but she left in a hurry and might have misplaced it. It could be just a copy."

"Then let's start by taking it to an insurance agent. One you can trust if there is such a thing."

"Call Paul and see if you get something from him and in the meantime, I'll look for an insurance agent or maybe a lawyer."

A teacher at school introduced Karina to her lawyer husband. He looked at the papers and immediately proclaimed them as copies. Somebody else had the originals.

"It looks like it was written without the knowledge of the owner and listed in their balance sheet. It's fraud, my dear. Re-insurance is the process in which insurance companies offset all or part of their risk through other insurance companies. These insurance companies are non-existent. Or . . . . a viatical settlement where the beneficial interests are sold or assigned to an investor who receives the full benefits when the insured dies. Paul might not know anything about this but it has definitely been collected. You have to report this to the police. Someone made a lot of money illegally and you may be involved by just knowing and not reporting it. Tell Paul about it because he would be confronted. The insurance industry can be the greatest victim of this fraud and they would be grateful. I don't really know exactly how it works. Go to an insurance agent and definitely the police."

"I don't want to get in the middle of this, my sister and ex-husband are involved or seems to be."

"I'm sorry my dear but it is your duty, your responsibility."

Karina couldn't believe her ears. That nice Paul, can't trust anyone. They can not get away with this. Poor Ana!

She drove home with all kinds of thoughts swimming in her head and whole body. She opened the door as the telephone rang.

"Yes?"

"This is Melina, my dear. I called Paul. He was as shocked as you and I. He says he doesn't know any Daniela, he hasn't heard or found anything about Ana—all still a mystery. He was sorry about you and Glenn but not surprised. Glenn's ethics had a lot to be desired. In other words I don' t think he is part of this unless he is a very good actor."

"Listen to this—the money was collected and most probably under fraudulent pretenses but we have to prove it. All I have is copies of a contract signed by Ana. I am afraid for Daniela and Glenn."

"You silly woman, don't be afraid for that devil of your sister and it looks to me that the two of them knew each other from way before. Let the police find out. Let me know what you do but don't lose sleep over it."

Karina decided to take the whole box to the police and let them do whatever was necessary. She couldn't get involved and she didn't know where to start looking for answers. She just hoped that it was a big misunderstanding. After all Ana's body has never been found.

She started planning her visit to Magnolia Meadows by checking magazines, furniture at different stores and other decoration schemes. She finally accepted her move and new life. She picked the telephone and made appointments to make arrangements for the necessary decisions. No more procrastination. This was probably going to be the longest bridge she would cross, all she needed was a lot of positive thinking.

Karina sat down with a cup of coffee to try to relax and write some lesson plans. The telephone shook her out of her intense preparation for the new semester.

"Hello, this is Detective Howard Lane. I was assigned to Ana Mendez' file.

Could we get together as soon as possible to answer some questions?"

"I really don't know anything. I just found the box and are pretty disturbed about it." Daniela is my sister and Glen was my husband. Paul is Glen's brother and that's all I can tell you."

"This involves you very much, Mrs. Bravo, I'm afraid." We better get together. This afternoon at 2:00 P.M.? I could come to your house or you can come to the precinct."

"Let's make it my house. I don't feel fit to drive and we would have more privacy."

The meeting went better than Karina expected. She answered everything that she could including the affair and what little she knew about Ana's disappearance.

"We found out that Ana was picked up from a ditch next to a wheel chair and taken to a hospital where she was treated for sustained injuries but she could not walk, hardly spoke and was suffering from amnesia. We think it was Ana but we are not so sure, when we tried to get to her, she was not there anymore and no one could tell us or wouldn't, where she had been taken. We feel she is still alive but doesn't know who she is. She has left no identification and apparently her face is somewhat disfigured so it makes it very hard to trace her even if she is found.

Karina could not stop the tears, she gave the policeman Paul's address and informed him that he didn't seem to be involved with Daniela at all.

"That is for me to decide. This looks quite complicated. I will get in touch with London police, talk to Paul and have a nice chat with Mr. Sheffield first, since he is still in business in Colorado. We have not been able to find your sister. Let's see if Mr. Sheffield knows where we can find her. Thank you very much. We will be in touch."

Karina breathed a sigh of relief. "I hope I don't have to be part of that mess. I do wish they find Ana soon, at least there is a possibility that she is still alive".

A knock at the door shocked her back into time.

"Getting ready to leave us?" Sylvia walked in softly.

"Well the time had to come sooner or later but I will be around at least another year if you would have me."

"Have you? We'd love to keep you but I know you have to keep moving forward." Sylvia looked so genuine!

"Right now I need your friendship more than ever." Maybe you will like the Meadows and move also, Is that a possibility?"

"Who knows? Who knows?"

Sylvia danced around with her arms swinging in the air in a teasing way.

Chapter 12

Fall was slipping gently into Magnolia Meadows with leaves beginning to change colors and the Meadows was cloaked in the Fall's rich paint. It was Karina's favorite season and Sylvia was in awe of the beauty of the different shades of red, yellow and orange that Mother nature had used to decorate the area. Karina was enjoying the winding roads as Sylvia enjoyed the burst of colors that painted the hills and meadows. They had to stop a couple of times as deer stopped to look at the car as if they had not seen one before, and after all it was their home. The dogwoods were spectacular and other hardwoods that they did not recognize were slowly changing from bright red to autumn orange.

"I've never seen such colors nor blend of trees in my entire life."

Sylvia was totally impressed and kept turning her head not to miss any beauty.

"Wait until you get to the minerals, crystals, lakes and the views are overwhelming."

As they approached the Meadows, a lot of energy started being felt in a familiar wave of expectancy as well as joy. The clouds started separating as if ordered by a major force revealing a calm, impressive, exquisite site that mystified them. It looked extraordinarily secured and hidden from the searching eyes of the traveler. The houses were blanketed by thick greenery and surrounded by mountain peaks of the Ozarks.

"Where is everything? There is nothing but nature's beauty."

Sylvia could not understand what Karina was moving into.

"You just wait my dear, you just wait." Karina teased Sylvia.

It seemed that Heaven had looked down on her nodding its approval of the scene she was beholding. They started seeing forms, houses, buildings and lots of rocks as well as crystals. They soon arrived at the registration center and Karina's new home. They spent the first day wandering around, meditating, orientating themselves and picking a lot of accessories, appliances, elevations etcetera. The sun streamed in and the shadows of the trees whizzed by showing the perfect place and she said to the realtor without a whisper of a doubt.

"This is it!"

After that, the rest was easy, just long and tiresome. It was as if she had been guided in such a way where she could find the right place to sit and contemplate, live her Metaphysical life that she so wanted. There was a magical energy that lifted her spirit and as such to be aware of her soul and purpose in life.

"I am going to be very happy here, Sylvia, for as long as I will stay. Can't I talk you into moving here also?"

"Oh no, I am a city girl. I would be crazy in a few months. No. I will visit you though. It's beautiful but feels like a cemetery to me."

Karina left everything to the realtor telling her that she could not come back until the move.

"Call me and we can decide over the telephone. I don't need to see what goes on and besides I don't know anything about building. I leave it in your hands and the guidance of the above."

The realtor shook her head in amazement but agreed.

The whole ordeal exhausted both Karina and Sylvia, mostly Karina because she had to make so many decisions and count her pennies. She was on a tight budget and she had to come up with large amounts of money in four installments. Her nerves were shot. They barely talked on their way back.

On arriving, the nurse informed them that a gentleman, a Mr. Glenn Sheffield had called and asked for Karina to please return the call as soon as she arrived.

'Not today' Karina said to herself. 'I can't deal with another situation right now.'

Two days passed and Glenn called again. Karina agreed to meet him for lunch.

"You have been the love of my life and still are. I made a big mistake, can't we try it again? We are perfectly bonded and have been crazy about each other."

Karina got very angry. How could he proclaim all the love when he had been cheating possibly for years.

She imagined violent scenes where he would suffer shame and misery. No, this is not right, must nudge all resentment in a different direction.

"No I don't feel that way anymore, Glenn. But I am very concerned about this problem with insurance fraud."

"This is what I want to talk about also. It was your sister's plan, together with John, but it just got out of hand. Apparently you had introduced her to Paul and Ana in London."

"I had not. I thought she was still in Isla Bonita when I was in Barcelona. Someone is lying big time."

"She lived in Florida while you were in Spain and she lived with an insurance man who got her involved in all kinds of dirty deals. We found each other in London and she asked me to drive her to my brother's. That's all I know. I met her again when she came to visit us and what happened between the two of us was a moment of weakness on my part. I don't know anything about this event. You have to help me clear it up."

"No, Glenn, I will not get involved. I do not understand what is going on. I can't end up finding out more information that will hurt me more than I have already been hurt. I am sorry. You have to find Daniela and resolve it between you two. I have a feeling that there is more to this than what you are saying. Explain it to the police."

With that said, she picked up her purse and left the table not touching her food.

She cried all the way home.

By the time she got home she had gone through her whole life with Daniela and the pain she had caused her over the years. She had rehashed every tidbit of conversation they had and how she twisted everything around to appear to be Karina's misgivings. She had forgiven her but she did not want her as part of her life anymore. And as far as Glenn was concerned, she was not going back to a bed of lies and sad memories that will be there possibly forever.

The sun peeked through the last shreds of clouds and by the time she reached her home blazing sunshine made the driveway glitter, the air felt clean and crystal clear and sunlight started to illuminate a divine future ahead of her. She felt closure on Glenn and Daniela's karma if that was what was.

Life had dealt her a bad card but she would show a poker face. People had always been attracted to secrets or what they can not figure out. She expected Glen to lie, if only for protection and she was not about to show him how hurt she was. Glen was angry and Karina figured that it was because he was caught. Perhaps he knew all along that Daniela was evil and he had no one to trust but hope that Karina would stand by him. Karina did not want anymore involvement and was fighting for herself not mentioning the whereabouts of Ana. She felt paralyzed and somewhat frightened but maybe after the conversation with Glen she could get rid of her doubts. Glen and Daniela were together in the whole incident with Ana. That was for sure. She took a hot shower and was asleep in seconds as her life with Glen danced in her head to just disappear into clouds of disappointment.

Police Report

A Neptune Lane woman became disoriented driving in the Meadows. Officers came to her aid and found an open bottle of Vodka in the back seat. When tested for alcohol, she was over the limit. She explained that she was playing Bridge and had a couple of glasses of wine. She did not know where the Vodka came from. Officers gave her a warning and helped her find her way home.

Chapter 13

Karina arrived at the Meadows and was immediately led to a copse of trees where she could get a hidden view of what was to be her residence. From the moment she set foot on the property, she was hooked. She was not going to be homesick here. The house was in a cul-de-sac with six houses before and six houses after hers. A small park-like in the middle made it looked like a chosen community especially for the twelve families who were living here.

Ten were couples and one more single, actually a widowed lady who took Karina under her care right from the start. They were all active in golf, tennis, Bridge, traveling and enjoyed a theater, walking trails and all sort of other activities. Barbara informed her of three single clubs she could join or enjoy whenever she felt like some company. Lots of churches were available for her to attend if she pleased. Gated, private and beautifully landscaped, the area offers an environment that is very appropriate for them to engage in healthy in and outdoor pools and spa with exercise programs. All kinds of social activities are available if you want to join. Actually one could be occupied from morning till night if one wanted to be.

Karina was not a joiner so she was not jumping into anything, not yet. She had to find a job first.

Sylvia had accompanied her and helped her with the unpacking and, buying furniture and subscribing to the utilities and necessary installations of telephones, mail box and bids for landscaping. It was a job and she was so lucky to have Sylvia helping her. Karina felt very lonely when she took Sylvia to the airport. It had been a month shared with laughter, apprehension and lots of love but her husband needed her and promising she would return soon, Sylvia bid so long to her good friend.

Barbara called to ask Karina to go downtown and get acquainted with the area. They stopped at a restaurant for lunch.

"This is my favorite restaurant and if we could be served, it would be perfect."

They ordered and found a table to sit. Barbara was full of all kinds of tips and information.

"I need a job, Barbara, and I intend to apply at the Board of Education since that is my field. I would like to have a job by September so I have to get busy."

"Fine, we can go there after lunch and get an application."

A tap on the shoulder made Karina turn around.

"Excuse me, I hear an accent and where ever there is an accent, there is a bilingual person. What other language do you speak?"

"Spanish and Italian. That's a very nice way to express your knowledge of culture and language." I am Karina Bravo, nice to meet you."

Replied Karina very surprisingly and polite.

"I am the Human Resources director for the Hospital and I need an interpreter like yesterday. Would you be interested in talking to me?"

A very well-dressed, attractive lady addressed her.

"Yes, of course, I never thought about interpreting but if it works for both of us, I'll be interested."

"Can you come for an interview next Wednesday morning? This is my card, Betsy Nelson."

Karina took the card in disbelieve.

"Thanks, I'll be there."

"I can't believe this has fallen on my lap. It must be right. What do you think?" Karina addressed Barbara with an admiration, question mark on her face.

"It could be great but let's apply for a teaching job anyway. That way you have choices."

Barbara was a little apprehensive but hopeful.

Karina felt so grateful and happy as they headed for the Board of Education.

Both interviews went smoothly and satisfying. The Board of Education offered a Teaching of Spanish position for September of the following year and she had to attend a couple of courses to get her license. That meant seven more months without a paycheck. The hospital offered an immediate position part time, but more money starting the following Monday. She decided to take the interpreter position and come September accept the teaching one . . . She was in seventh heaven. She went home singing as she thanked the universe for the good luck. Karina notified her kids about the latest happenings and they both breathed a sigh of relief.

Barbara invited her to attend a meeting of her singles' club and she reluctantly accepted. She needed to start socializing sometime. This was as good as anything.

She prepared a batch of cookies to take for dessert as dinner was part of the plan. They met every Saturday night at 5:30 PM. Early to bed and early to rise was apparently the mode in the community. Karina found a chair at the same table as Barbara and a gentleman sat next to her. A new arrival was very popular right away especially if she was halfway nice looking.

"I want you to know that you are sitting next to the best catch available here. I have plenty of money, not to mention that all the women are after me, but I like you. How lucky can you get! Now tell me about you."

Karina went insane with what she considered an insult.

"If you do not leave that chair right this minute, I will leave. One can build monuments to your self centeredness, sir"

Barbara tried to stop her but she had gotten up and was heading for the door as everybody looked at her in awed.

"Wait, don't pay any attention to this jerk, nobody else does. Let's sit someplace else and enjoy the dinner and meet nice people."

The evening was ruined for Karina. She thought she would meet nothing but nice men who would be interested in having a friend. She was not into dating nor marriage, not for now anyway. The other women were not too friendly and kept away from her. She felt misplaced and very uncomfortable. She prayed for the evening to end and kept the small talk to the best of her tolerance.

Barbara tried to calm her apologizing for Charlie and promising a better experience next time.

"Don't judge everyone from this experience. Give them another chance."

It was such a disappointment to Karina that she started crying non stop.

"I just want to be home, let's go, please." It isn't your fault. You are trying to make me acceptable, it's me. I am sorry and thanks."

So ended her first encounter with the singles club, one of them anyway. She kissed Barbara good night. She couldn't go to sleep so she sat at the kitchen table with a cup of tea and proceeded to make a budget accentuating the three most important categories to be sure she was financially stable: bare necessities (food, shelter, transportation and health care), flexible spending items (clothing, entertainment, gifts and contributions), and luxuries, (travel and other splurges). Next, she wanted to determine what level of spending her resources would support. If she watched her income carefully, she could do it with the hospital job and she would have more time to rest, maybe socialize and visit her children. Once she started getting social security, she would have some extra money for savings. Karina was ready for a new beginning. If this did not work she could always teach come September.

The street where she lived had their annual barbeque and she was invited. The couples were all very nice and very neighborly but mostly the women were curious to know where she was coming and who she was. They offered the different churches for Sunday visits and they all proclaimed their redeeming qualities. Karina gracefully thanked them and expressed her belief system in a very religiously acceptable way.

Rosemarie was very friendly with all the men. Grace was on her third marriage and from her conversation, ready for the next. Ruth protected her doctor husband from all the others especially Karina. Beverly was strange and Karina believed that she and her partner were living together. Kathy did not look happily married and was cold and detached. Karina made a promise to herself that she would stay friendly but not scrambled.

Being single made it difficult to be very friendly because like everywhere else, she was a threat to both married and single women. This was not any different, to her disappointment. Karina was counting on a very relaxed atmosphere where there would be no competition or fears. There were more women than men making it a man's paradise since the women used all their guile to attract the available men and the men did not fight it. It was a tsunami of a competition. Karina kept thinking positively and promised to enjoy life in the Meadows.

That Sunday she got up early and drove around to get acquainted with the area. She took a couple of wrong turns and of course got lost but ended next to a place that Barbara had mentioned which was good for a light lunch. She decided to go in and try it. She ordered a fish sandwich and soon realized that everything in the Meadows was fried even the bread. She was going to be careful with her weight. She smiled to herself as she enjoyed the pleasant atmosphere of country life.

She was able to find her way around from there on realizing that the orange line marked on some roads took one to the main road and from there to one's residence. She turned into a main road and drove what seemed forever, until she saw some familiar signs that took her home. She had to do this a couple of times until she felt comfortable. Next Sunday she was going to try visiting the nearby town. What she had seen was very quaint and hospitable, exactly her cup of tea. She knew she was going to enjoy it while hoping that it would stay country looking, for her enjoyment and comfort.

Police Report

A Moon Lane woman called to report an accident on her street. It appeared the driver passed out behind the wheel. He was issued citations for DWI, third offense, and refusal to submit. He was arrested and charged with possession of Marijuana and drug paraphernalia, careless and prohibited driving.

Chapter 14

The unpacking is finally over and all put away on the tiled lined shelves. The to do list is getting shorter and most items crossed out. The needle on Karina's emotional tank was on empty and the stress on full. Even though she had simplified her life, she was not totally worry free. She told herself that worry was nothing but a prayer of doom but her responsibility did not let her escape from it. Her house was not paid off, neither was her car. Even though 40% of her income was secure, it was not enough, she had to be able to cut a fifth of her spending if hard times came. Actually she had not been able to open a savings account. This was a big concern to her. She accepted the fact that she had to work indefinitely, at least part time.

The interpreter job at the hospital came as a present from heaven. This way she could stay engaged and support a comfortable lifestyle. Next on her list was the purchase of a long-term care insurance. She was not going to be a burden to her kids.

Karina served herself a cup of tea and looked through the entertainment, clubs and activities offered. She decided she would join some club to meet new friends and possibly a Bridge group for a starter. It would be nice to get season tickets to the theater. She revised her options and made plans rather than allow a big problem to bubble up. Yet, what appears as an impossible dream could indeed be nothing but a mirage. Part budget, part road map, she sat down to plan her strategy.

First she would call the kids to come and get whatever they wanted or could use. Karina was ready to de-clutter her life. Some things she wanted to retain for practical or sentimental reasons but there was a lot of stuff that she did not need anymore and really wouldn't miss so, what the kids did not want, would be sold, donated or trashed . . . This left her with an increase sense of freedom and mental space to fill with new activities.

The door bell brought her back to reality. Barbara came to offer her help and invite her to have dinner with her and two other girls, and maybe play a little Bridge.

"You had such a bad start with that jerk, I want to offer you a new beginning. Since you start to work Monday, today is your day to relax and enjoy."

"Barbara you have been such a dear. I had already forgotten the episode and wouldn't mention it again. There is one of those everywhere. I want to believe that he is the only one here."

"Not that good my dear. You will probably meet others, so now you are prepared. At least no one will attack you. They are lambs in wolf clothing."

"I have been reading the police reports and I get kind of bothered that we have people like that in this kind of environment. Are those reports for real?"

"Unfortunately yes. We have all kinds and the residents do drink a lot. That combined with poor eyesight and slow reflexes form a dangerous combination. It's funny women drink more than the men. They feel they are away from the city and they are entitled to relaxation and do stupid combinations to achieve it. I know a woman who mixes tranquilizers with Vodka."

"That's crazy! Is she trying to kill herself?"

"Not only that, she is a nurse. Can you imagine such stupidity? She is always in a trance-like behavior . . . But I bought tickets to the next show at the theater, they are very reasonable and they are pretty good considering that this is a small community. They are for next Saturday so plan on it."

"Let me pay for mine, you are being wonderful but I don't want you to spend your money, we are all watching our budgets."

"You are on and now let's go play some Bridge."

Dinner turned out to be very good and enjoyable. Karina immediately realized that she had to watch what she ate in fear of gaining weight. It was too easy to do so. It was a major form of entertainment. They leisurely drank the rest of the wine and happily left for a night of Bridge, the favorite past-time in her new way of life.

Bridge had been put together by a group of widows. Even though Karina was not a recent widow she was once and so was invited to join which she did right away. The evening was a real pleasure and she was able to put aside all her apprehensions. It seemed all of the women were pretty much in her same shoes.

"Welcome to paradise" laughingly said Alice, a widow that had not been able to cope too well with her new condition: she apparently still missed her husband and her married life.

"I still cry thinking about my Howard" she wiped a tear from her eye as she hugged Karina in an effort to show her acceptance of her.

"Are you thinking of finding a new man, Karina, you're so beautiful, it would not be hard. Wait until men see you and the other women push you aside as they compete with the few men available." Grace was kind of catty but she meant no harm.

"We have a casserole brigade, a woman dies and all these women rush to bring all kinds of food to the widower in hopes of getting his attention. First come, first served kind of an unspoken pledge." Diane giggled as she said her bit.

"Sounds like a very interesting life for all." Replied Karina as she pulled back her chair to join her Bridge table. Two hearts" She proudly announced.

Police Report

Betty Caddie was issued a citation for failure to yield when she pulled in front of oncoming traffic to turn off of Meteor Way to Comet Drive Her car sustained approximately $10,000 in damages. The car that hit her car sustained $12,000 in damages. Both cars had to be towed from the accident.

Chapter 15

Karina arrived to a very tense environment of nurses and doctors running back and forth trying to cope with the overflow of patients. This, not being her expertise, overwhelmed her right away as she moved nervously to report for work.

'Can't be any worse than teaching at the inner city schools' she told herself. 'I need to learn my surroundings and what is expected of me.'

As she was trying to find her way around, a security agent approached her noticing her interpreter badge on her chest.

Pointing to a scared lady he mumbled:

"She apparently is very sick, she keeps saying emergency, emergency but can't tell me the problem. I don't know where to take her, can you help?"

Karina put her hands on the lady's shoulder to calm her down. She asked her in Spanish:

"What is the problem? What can I do for you? Are you hurting? We are here to help you. It's going to be all right, you'll see."

"I am not sick "she replied in Spanish. "I left my car in the emergency parking lot and I can't find my way around. I am here to visit a friend."

Karina explained the situation to the security guard who proceeded to show her the way while scratching his head in disbelieve or maybe relieve.

'This is going to be a very special job and funny to boot. I like helping others and these people need help.' She thought to herself.

Karina walked the long corridor to report for her new job. She was going to work part-time. Three days a week 8:30a.m. to 3:30p.m. She needed to be available for the whole hospital but was going to be based at the clinic where they needed her the most. This suited Karina perfectly since she would make enough money to augment her income and plenty of time to visit her kids and have some kind of social life.

The clinic served women with low incomes and no health insurance. The staff consisted of the director, one receptionist, two nurses and a nurse practitioner. Five doctors took turns offering their services. and one financial advisor took care of the Medicaid services. It was definitely understaffed but the care was excellent. All were very well informed and were dedicated. Even though the army of patients were not the best to deal with. They were demanding, disrespectful, would not follow advice and actually did as they pleased without regard for the safety of their babies.

The foreign patients were not in this category, most were very grateful and followers of the regulations imposed on them by the doctors and staff.

Karina gave her services wherever she was needed being the only interpreter in the whole hospital. This took her everywhere and when her beeper rang, she moved fast to the place she was summoned to.

"Mrs. Bravo, Would you report to room 302? I have a patient who refuses to undress and be examined."

The voice of the floor manager sounded frustrated and nervous.

"I'll be right over."

Karina signed off and rushed to the elevator that would take her to the 3rd floor. On arrival, she was directed to this girl sitting on a chair and not moving.

"What is the problem? How can I help you? We need to examine you and I can stay with you while you are checked."

“I am not undressing or getting in that bed because there is nothing wrong with me.”

“Then, why are you here?”

Karina asked kind of puzzled.

“I brought my friend who has passed out in the bathroom while you play musical chairs trying to get me in bed. She is throwing up, is running a temperature and can’t stand up for very long.”

She explained in Spanish with relieve at hearing Karina speaking her language.

The nurse and the manager ran into the bathroom to find a girl laying flat on her back, shaking with vomit coming out of her mouth.

Karina bid all farewell and after filling out the necessary paperwork, returned to her post.

Penny, the receptionist, a serious, religious soul greeted her with:

“Melanie has been in room 5 for the past half hour with Doctor Garret and I don’t know what she is doing because they were asking for you. Maybe you should knock at the door.”

Melanie was going through a divorce. After fifteen years of marriage, her husband informed her that he preferred men and had a boyfriend. He wanted her to know it but he loved his family and wanted to stay married to her. Melanie tried to abide by his wishes but it became more and more difficult to live up to the lie that her marriage had become or maybe always was. She shriveled at the thought of her not having known the truth all this time, trusting and loving while he made love to her disgustingly. She walked into the office one day and exploded with all the pain she had been enduring and proceeded to sue for divorce. After that she had become a real player maybe out of anger or vengeance.

Karina was about to knock when a disheveled Melanie came out and closed the door behind her.

"I have a girl in the lab room, she is afraid of needles and won't let us draw blood. Find out what this is all about, please."

Karina walked to the lab to find Maria crying. She was terrified of needles, she explained. Karina talked to her while holding her hands and spoke gently and softly:

"We need the blood to find out about your health so that we can take care of you and your baby. You must be strong. I'll hold your hand and you look the other way and before you know it will all be over, For your baby—OK?"

Maria nodded and the blood was drawn with no more problems.

Melanie ran her fingers through her hair in an effort to put it back in place.

"Thank you, you are a life saver."

The rumor was that she was having an affair with Dr. Garrett but they both denied any connections, after all Dr. Garrett was a married man but known for his escapades with the nurses. Karina did not want to go there. The receptionist handed her the telephone. "It's the Cancer Center."

As Karina accepted the telephone, Carol, the nurse practitioner, came out of the room she was attending in, and asked Penny to call security. "Tell them to hurry" she said with a lump in her throat voice.

Lois, an experienced nurse assistant, rushed to her aid.

Carol was always calm and collected. She didn't show any disturbed emotions or turmoil in her life. She had mastered the art of talking to others as she documented information in the computer without missing one word or procedure done: accurate and explicit.

"Where did you get the antibiotic?"

Carol interrogated the patient who was laying on the examining table and was not very cooperative.

"In the feed store-" she nastily responded,

"Is there anyone there licensed to do that?"

"Are you crazy? You just pick it from the shelves"

"Well, I hate to tell you this but you are taking an antibiotic for horses"

"No way, may I see someone else?"

"Get undressed, wear this gown and I'll be back to examine you."

As Carol inserted the speculum in her vagina, she felt a lump that did not let the speculum penetrate and to her surprise found a bag with cocaine in it.

"Get security" Carol asked Melanie.

"What has happened?" Melanie was astounded.

"I found a bag of cocaine inside her"—pointing at the patient laying on the bed.

"Ridiculous, I have no clue of how that got there."

The patient was really angry and demanding.

"But now that you found it, it is mine and I am asking you give it to me."

"It was yours", said Carol," now it belongs to us. I am calling the doctor and you respond to this assault on your baby's health with a good excuse."

The security and people in charge of criminal acts showed up and Carol left them with the patient and proceeded to write her report. Carol was very dedicated and in love with her profession. She never complained and did a very thorough job. Married to a giant of a man whom she adored, her main interest in life was her family and her job had become a pretty close second.

Her husband was a counselor at a local High School, they had two children and enjoyed a very standard, average American life. She was quiet and reserve, also knew her job to perfection. Her job was a joy to her.

Karina was shocked but was told that it was a repeated episode, unfortunately. She left for the Cancer center concerned and apprehensive. This was another side of life that she had not experienced. She prayed for guidance.

Jamie Lynn, the patient's advocate was waiting for her at the front desk. Jamie showed power and leadership the minute one met her. She handed Karina a bunch of papers.

"Here, my dear, Mr. Garcia has three months to live at the most. He has lost his job as you can imagine. He has four children and a wife who cares for them. We need to call the schools and get some aid soon. Here are some telephone numbers to guide you and call me as soon as you find something."

With that said, she went back to her office. Karina looked at the sad family and asked them how they felt about returning to Mexico. Their faces lit up but there was a small problem. Mr. Garcia had a trial pending for driving under the influence of alcohol. Well that was a start for Karina. She picked her papers, took some information from The Garcia's and bid them good bye until she found a solution to their problem.

Two weeks later the family was on their way to Mexico. Karina felt very satisfied and happy for them. It was 4:30 P.M. by the time she returned to the clinic. She picked up her belongings and left for the day.

Karina had to stop to see Audrey, a cute thirty-two year old blonde, divorced with two children. Audrey was teaching the complicated use of the computer to Karina who called herself computer illiterate. Karina had helped Audrey get a registration clerk job at the hospital and in return Audrey helped her with classes. Audrey was fighting a nasty divorce from her lawyer husband who wanted custody of the children. Audrey lived in the Meadows where her parents lived so that they could help her with the care of the kids. Karina unwillingly went to her class.

Police Report

A Mars lane woman said a man was driving on Sunset Drive near the RV park entrance when a deer entered the roadway. The driver swerved to miss the deer, overcorrected and the car ended up on its side in a ditch. The driver said he was fine but the car was a total loss.

Chapter 16

Karina arrived at her home to find cars and neighbors on the street. Some of the people were outside congregated and talking, others were coming out of Jessica's house. She ran to see what was happening.

It looks like John has had a massive heart attack. Jessica is getting ready to take him to the hospital or wherever he needs to go.

"But he was fine this morning"—Karina's voice was shaking.

"It happened suddenly. He was in the garage, when he did not respond to Jessica's calls, she went looking for him and found him laying on the floor. The paramedics are on the way."

Elaine was really shaken.

Karina went into the house and hugged Jessica who was stunned.

"I'm here, we are all here, you just go with him, and we will make the necessary calls to the family."

"Thanks, I need to let the boys know right away."

The paramedics arrived and took him in the ambulance but he died on the way to the hospital. Barbara and Karina had followed the ambulance and helped Jessica to make the necessary arrangements with the funeral home. The boys were on their way and Karina offered to pick them up at the airport. Barbara took Jessica back home where Jessica's sister was waiting.

It was a very sorrowful family reunion and Karina felt it was very private and she hugged Jessica so long.

Karina relived all the pain she endured when Enrique died and she felt the usual guilt of not being there to be with him at least through his last hours. She wiped the tears and proceeded to prepare something to eat and make some cookies for Jessica. The telephone interrupted her thoughts. It was Alice, one of the girls in the street.

"I want to have you over for dinner and meet some friends of ours; this of course after the incident with Jessica is taken care of. I am afraid Jessica is not going to suffer too much, she is resilient and too much in love with herself. She will be fine."

"How about Saturday two weeks from today?"

"Let me check my calendar, it should be ok."

Karina accepted but surprised at such a sudden, mysterious invitation.

"Good, their names are Anne and Ronald Phillips and it is going to be a welcome meeting. See you then. 6:00 o'clock dinner at 7:00."

Jessica went on a trip to Mexico to try to erase the death episode as she called it. Life apparently went on for her with no pain, no regrets. She had already attended some parties and had joined the grief group mainly to meet others in her same position or so she proclaimed. The people on their street were not too happy with her behavior and certainly all felt bad for the boys who were still mourning.

Two weeks later the street saw the arrival of Luke who moved in with Jessica causing quite a stir.

"Everyone is saying that she knew him from before when her husband was still alive" commented Betty on the telephone to Karina.

"I don't want to judge, I know nothing about it." Responded Karina. "She must be very lonely."

"She is going crazy, she has been talking about not wearing any underwear."

"Hard to believe. No one talks like that." Karina could not believe her ears.

"Oh I can tell you, you don't know Jessica. I wish she would move away.

"That man is married, I can see problems ahead."

"Guess he was married but he got a divorce and went away to Alaska to celebrate and stayed in Jessica's house happy as a lark. Jessica is exuberant."

Karina woke up not feeling too well but she pushed herself to get dressed and go to work. Dr Grant was waiting for her.

"Can I borrow you for a minute?"

"Of course" Karina perked up.

"This girl has met with a POD and needs immediate care. Give her the details on the procedure and she must do it as soon as possible. Tell her that her partner needs treatment at the Health Clinic and give her the instructions to take to him."

"What is a POD? I have never heard of it." Karina asked apprehensively.

"It's what I call it: Penis of death. She contacted a venereal disease. In her case Syphilis."

Karina still could not understand these situations and felt like throwing up but she pulled herself together.

Penny informed Karina that Medical Records needed her and she nodded as she started on her way to see what they needed.

Jane had that desperate, frustrated look that she often showed when she could not do her job because she did not understand. She handed Karina a form.

It was all filled out wrongly. Karina looked at it and called the patient. Maiden name-the patient put her mother's name

Residence—Oaxaca, Mexico

Sex—Fine

Highest grade completed—C

Karina filled out a new form with right information.

"Didn't you get any help with this?"

"No, I was afraid to ask so, I did what I could."

Most of the foreign patients were afraid to ask, fearful of immigration.

"You have to come to sign this new one that I have done for you."

With that said she took the long walk to the emergency room where someone had been in a car/ motorcycle accident.

A male nurse met Karina at the desk.

"Don't go there. You don't want to see the patient. We need for you to call his mother and explained what happened. He probably will not survive."

This was the part of the job that Karina hated but knew that just hearing her voice, in the mother's language, was a consolation in itself.

It had been a long day and she did not feel any better. She decided to cancel the dinner party.

"Alice, can I take a rain check on your dinner party? I am not feeling well, looks like a bad cold because my throat and body hurt. It is best that I take care of it during the week-end so that I don't miss too much work."

"Oh, I'm sorry, I'll bring some soup. Yes, of course we can do it next month when the Phillips are available".

"Thanks."

Karina took a hot shower and prepared for bed. She could not help wonder why the insistence of Alice about meeting the Phillips.

'She must know something I don't know or wants me to know. I hope is nothing unpleasant.'

The door bell rang and Alice was her smiling self and holding the container with some chicken soup which Karina gratefully accepted.

"Alice, who are the Phillips?"

"Oh you'll love them. Ann is from Isla Bonita so I think you will have a lot to share and you need that connection. Ronald is a therapist and has his practice near here. They have lived here for five years, guess they met in London . . . . But she can tell you all about it when you see them. Take care and call me if you need anything".

With that said she hugged Karina farewell.

Karina now felt a curiosity to meet the Phillips and could hardly wait to make the connection. She took the soup to the kitchen and went for a short shower. As she let the water run over her achy body she reminisce about her time in Spain and the friendship with Ana and Melina. She missed them. She took a couple of sips of the delicious soup and wrapped herself in a blanket in front of the television when the telephone disturbed her newly obtained comfort. It was her friend Audrey.

"Guess what happened?" a very shaky voice came out loud and clear. "Max got married to his lawyer. Surprise?"

"No, not really" answered Karina in a not too compassionate voice. "Maybe now he will leave you alone."

"Let's have lunch Monday and you can tell me all about it. I am not feeling very well."

"Oh I am sorry. Anything I can do?"

"No, not really. I need some rest. Twelve noon at the cafeteria and you can tell me all about it. Good night Audrey."

Audrey was not the average middle class girl, surprisingly enough coming from such a religious background. Her parents wanted to marry her off to wealth and she obeyed and followed their advice. Karina thought she was way too liberal, but accepted her without question. Hope all was well with her and she turned the TV to her favorite program. Karina felt that maybe she was paying a heavy price for her computer lessons since Audrey had become a big problem, typical of the young people living in the Meadows. Most of the young people were looking for a husband that would give them financial security, but were not mature enough to handle the age difference.

Karina felt responsible for Audrey and hoped that Audrey would listen to her and put her life together without the strings that she had attached herself to. She put her mind into the program in the television trying to forget that she and Audrey were meeting the next day.

Police Report

A Mars Way woman asked officers to help her find a car she was supposed to escort to Uranus Dr. following Bingo at the Big Star Center. The car was not in the parking lot. Officers called the missing driver's daughter. The woman said her mother had not returned home and that she had bad eyesight and had left her hearing aids and was a diabetic . . . Officers found a car traveling 20mph on Milky Way Road. The car was weaving and occasionally stopping. The officers stopped her and advised her not to drive anymore.

Chapter 17

Karina woke up really refreshed: the rest and soup did their job. She intended to stay put all week-end. She poured herself a cup of coffee and sat by the window to admire the coming of Fall. October, being her favorite month of the year tugged tightly on a cool morning cover as piles of orange leaves reflected its coming. Trees of gold, red, yellow start reflecting on the many lakes in the Meadows. The weather and the beauty of the landscape invite to a picnic as Autumn's palette adorns the gardens. Amid the streets and between the houses, the Meadows meld into the rich and lush season. The skies are so blue, one wants to look at them all day in this Autumn splendor.

Karina is always amazed and can not overlook the most beautiful of the landscape—the weed broom sedge. It's the weed that turns the whole country side the color of ripe pumpkins creating an ocean-like of grass that has been stroked by the wind. Karina is reminded of her annual Thanksgiving visit with her kids, one which she always looks forward to. This year they are meeting at Nicolas' new house. Karina had not seen it and was looking forward to meeting the new baby girl. Adriana had made a new life in California with her doctor husband and would also join them.

She poured herself another cup of coffee as the door bell rang. Barbara had come to see how she was. Barbara was always a big comfort to her. Karina served her a cup of coffee and they sat to chat and gossip. Barbara wanted Karina to stay. She really liked her but was afraid that she did not understand the ways of the residents.

"Remember they come from the generation when having a drink before dinner was the only and accepted way to relax."

"Except that in retirement they have tripled the doses. It's dangerous, Barbara. One of them can kill one of us or both!"

"Others, my dear have all they ever wanted and couldn't afford. The golf course, tennis, country club etc"

"The problem is that it is the way that is every place else. If you are single and half way good looking, you are going to be left out."

"I think you are right. We have to do the best with what we have. There is always a Jessica. She takes what she wants regardless of consequences."

"You know Beverly is getting married again to Clare Watters' ex husband"

"But weren't they best friends?"

"You see? Yes, and he is divorcing Clare to marry Beverly. Apparently they had been seeing each other for quite a while even as she was married to Scott. Beverly doesn't waste any time, my dear. I understand that she asked Scott to move out, gave him a couple of thousands of dollars and moved David in. Clare is furious and is suing for quite a bit of money which I understand Beverly is willing to settle out of court. This is Beverly's fourth marriage here at the Meadows because she came in with her husband who died two years later."

"Is it true that the Big Star Center is not renting rooms sparingly anymore?

Someone said that they found out that both men and women rent rooms by the hour and have sexual activities unbeknown to the mates and the director."

"I heard something like that also and that is why the Hospital is offering the seminar on sexual behavior and protection. Most of the residents don't realize that now we have all these diseases that were not around when we were dating a long time ago."

"Life is interesting at The Meadows. I'll say."

"You also have to be careful who you get involved with. A lot of these men are looking for a nurse or a purse. I know of this girl who had lost her first husband (a doctor) the first year after they moved here. She was a secretary and did not make a lot of money but her husband left her well provided for. She owned their home and two condos, had no debts and received some income from investments . . . She soon remarried and eventually let her new husband persuade her to replace her paid for residence for a more expensive, bigger one which she had to finance. As a consequence of this he became a co-owner of such residence. She used some of her savings to finance a business that her dear new husband owned. With lots of promises and loving he talked her into changing the titles of the condos into jointly held properties. It was not too long after that that he sued her for divorce."

“The rat! Why do we women need so desperately to have a man around? It’s so sad. We all battle with two fears, of being abandoned and of being possessed. We want to be close to someone to not feel lonely and be connected and at the same time we want freedom and distance from the one we love. Sex and the emotional and physical closeness meets the need for closeness but it makes detachment very difficult thus the need to feel complete but not alone. Marriage, or a long term relationship is the safest place to be, even though it can be boring after a long period of time. Exchanging partners doesn’t solve your problem.”

“I also know very devoted couples that are very happy together. Not many though.”

“Are you going to work Monday?”

“Yes I better.”

“Do you feel up to do something Saturday? Have you met that girl that Alice wants to get in touch with you?”

“No. I’m really curious. I understand she is also from Isla Bonita I am looking forward to meeting her. As far as doing something Saturday, why don’t you come over for dinner and a movie? I don’t think I should push it.”

“It’s a date.” Barbara hugged Karina.” I love you dear, take care.”

Police Report

A Neptune Lane woman said she and her husband were awakened by their barking dogs and got up to find an unknown elderly woman standing in their living room. She appeared in good health and spirits but was unable to say where she lived. Once identified, the lost woman's husband said that he had just discovered her missing and had called the police.

Chapter 18

The sun was late coming out and the sky clear but pale; the wind whipped Karina's body as if pouring out of the North like the exhaust from a jet plane. The temperature had a sudden drop and it felt more like Winter than Fall. Karina goes back into the house to get a coat. She picked up her small leather cap, looked at herself in the hall mirror and confidently said to herself:

'Amazing how much dignity can be had in a hat, once on your head, it makes you feel superior, kind of in control, secured.'

She closed the door behind her and headed for the hospital.

Heather was waiting for her to take her to surgery. The patient had asked for Karina to be present. Carmen laid in sheer expectancy of what was about to happen. The patient had four children and she didn't want anymore but her husband did believing that God had a say on it . . . Karina translated the proceedings as she held her hand to make her feel confident in a world so foreign to her. Carmen was having her second cesarean section and on opening the area, the Doctor murmured:

"The uterus is extremely thin."

Doctor Keller proceeded to cut. After all was done he just asked:

"Shall I tie the tubes as talked about?"

Carmen happily squeezed Karina's hand in approval as a smirk of a smile formed on her face. She had won this battle.

Karina left Carmen asleep and ran to ER where she had been summoned. There had been an accident in one of the saw mills. The young man laying down was covered with blood and a piece of wood was stuck in his stomach. Karina took a couple of steps back, it was not a pleasant scene to watch. She stood back as nurses and doctors ran back and forth trying to help him and ease his pain. He needed immediate surgery and Karina explained to him what was going on. She took all the necessary information about relatives, work, insurance. He asked Karina to come close and he whispered:

"If my organ there Senora?"

Karina was not shocked anymore, so she pulled the sheet, looked and said:

"Yes, it's there but there are more important things to worry about."

"That's a matter of opinion" was his reply as he twisted in pain.

He was wheeled to surgery. Karina had lost her appetite but met with the other girls for lunch.

One o'clock came fast enough. The financial advisor needed Karina. The patient was very upset since she did not understand exactly why she could not have another ultrasound.

"You are allowed two ultrasounds and you have maxed the Medicaid allowance. You have to pay for this one if you want it but actually you don't need another one."

She accepted her lot and left after thanking Karina.

Dr. Garrett reluctantly and with apprehension opened the door. He was not sure of who he was seeing or what the problem, if any, was . . . He scratched his butt to face the computer which he hated. The patient had a history of drug abuse and she also smoked.

Louise came in to help.

"Take off everything and put on this gown. We will return in a couple of minutes."

On their return, the doctor talked to her about the dangers of drug abuse and smoking but she just laughed. He looked down on her with her bare breasts pointing up to the ceiling and he dropped his chewing gum right between the two phenomenal specimens. He said, embarrassed:

"I'm so sorry!"

The girl looked at him flirting and joking:

"You pick it up", as she pushed her breasts together with her hands.

The doctor rapidly left the room leaving Louise to handle the situation.

Louise came out of the room laughing and teasing Dr. Garrett. It was the funny tale of the day as they all regarded Dr Garrett as the epitome of self confidence . . .

Karina answered the telephone that was handed to her.

"Hello! Bueno!"

"Karina this is Alice, I'm sorry to bother you at work but I need to confirm this before the day is over."

"No problem" answered Karina somewhat apprehensive

"How about dinner two weeks from this Saturday.? Ann and Ron will be in town and then they are leaving for New York."

"That sounds great. I hope it works out this time. I am so looking forward to meeting the Phillips. It's a date."

Karina wrapped it up and headed for home. At home finally, she took a long hot bath and relaxed watching a new soap opera. She would be free tomorrow. Wednesday was her favorite day of the week just like Friday was when she was working full time. She woke up refreshed and ready to tackle the different chores that the house demanded.

It was a cool morning but the fireplace took the edge off the early Autumn air. Coffee and an assortment of fruits and pastry fueled her morning. She put on her sweats and started the scheduled jobs of the day. She was also attending a program at the Entertainment Center with her Singles group and Sunday, she and Barb were invited to go sailing in the morning.

She was beginning to enjoy life at the Meadows with all its oohs and aahs and lavish praises as only Southerners can layer and sound sincere.

Karina liked her small home. It was just right for this time in her life. The clean lines and easy care was what she wanted. One could see almost the whole house from the living room. The Tuscan style look coordinated with the outside. It was her casual, comfortable retreat full of trees with a hammock leisurely available in the patio for her to read or just nap.

She practiced Yoga and meditation an hour a week so she had less tension, more energy and general stress relief. It was a way of life with her and after that everything was approachable.

Barb called interrupting her worst chore, making her bed, inviting her to a get together at her home before the concert.

"Can you make your Mint Julep?"
"Of course. I must remind you that it has Bourbon."
"I knew it had some liquor. We'll take it easy."
"Yes, mint, sugar and a little club soda."

"Sounds delightful.
See you at 5:00 PM"

With all chores finished, Karina sat down with a face masque on and called Adriana.

"Are you ready for Thanksgiving?"

"Not quite Mom. Both kids are sick and I'm beginning to get a sore throat.

When one has kids, we are always exposed to their germs that they pick up at school, playground or others playmates. It is not uncommon.

Well, I'm trying hard to be well so we can make it to Nicolas'. You know how much I like Thanksgiving."

"You have a month to take care of you all."

"Yeah but we keep passing it around! We need the vacation for a weary family escaping the everyday, house, hospital, school world. We made reservations at a nearby Dude Ranch, famous among equestrians but wonderfully undiscovered by everyone else. Christopher wants to go fishing while we enjoy a roaring fire. Are you game?"

"Sounds great!. Nicolas says that he built tree houses and are only accessible by boat. I expect to hike a little but around the cottage."

"Oh, Mom I can hardly wait. I haven't seen you for so long. I am looking forward to Karen's freshly baked breakfasts and Nicolas' barbecues."

"Your house should be finished for next year. You have a lot to catch up to. I just love to be with the grandchildren and watch them enjoy themselves. It gives me a relaxed sense of responsibility, not like when I was taking care of you kids."

"Hija, I have to go."

"I know Mom, me too. Is life in the Meadows still agreeable to your wants and needs? Remember you can always come here."

"I know. I'm getting used to it. I am meeting a couple, she is from Isla Bonita and I am really looking forward to share our journeys. I'll call next week."

Karina started to review the experience lived with Ana's disappearance. Nothing had been resolved and she still hoped for a clue on her case. She just could not have disappeared into thin air. Karina couldn't shake off the feeling of uneasiness and frustration, something was stuck in her throat and she could not release it. She didn't know why it had come to her now. Maybe because of her talk with Alice. She proceeded toward her bedroom, she felt fuzzy but was counting on a good night sleep.

Karina had not totally recuperated from her big night out with the girls but reported to work as usual. At twelve sharp she headed for the cafeteria to meet with Audrey.

Audrey appeared very disturbed or maybe just jealous that her ex had married the lawyer so fast and that meant to her that they were seeing each other for a long time.

"It's ok I guess, because I am seeing a new guy. My parents introduced me to Karl, he is an old friend. His wife had died and in typical Meadows style, every one he knew came over with a casserole. Audrey's parents brought cookies—his favorite but they waited until after the funeral. Two weeks later Karl and Audrey were a twosome. Karl was twenty-five years older than Audrey.

"Are you overlooking the age difference or accepting It?"

"I'm accepting it. He thinks young and is great with the kids and I would have no money worries if I got him to marry me."

"Looks like it is a plan". Karina listened in awed and proposed avenues to go being careful not to appear judgmental.

They hugged and went back to their respective jobs.

Karina kept juggling the situation in her head, she just could not understand that way of thinking, Marriage or even a close relationship, to her, meant being in love, cooperation, understanding, respect, but it had not worked for her so who was she to complain?

She put Audrey out of her mind and put her energy on the work at hand.

Police Report

A Neptune Lane woman told the police that an unidentified person had left a message on her son's Edwin cell phone saying they were going to burn down her home recently identified as a Meth lab. The police will investigate.

Chapter 19

Karina had a wonderful time, she truly enjoyed the evening but there was always that need to discuss her feelings, fears, longings—someone to give back without her being judged, envied or portrayed as different. There was always a chasm between the people she met and herself; there were no mirrors. She couldn't get to know anyone enough and she could not burden Barb with the weight of her dreams. Barb was good for her but the intimacy was not there—not like what she had with Melina and Ana. She did not know if it was culture or her own fears. Karina missed her friends a lot. She could cry but she simply didn't think she could do anymore of that. She also missed her children even though she was glad they had made lives of their own. Glen was still in her heart and she still hoped he would come and make everything right and save her from drowning in the sea of guilt that she felt on and off and stand tall by her side. She felt very nostalgic and she realized she was still very bruised.

She felt confused and aroused. Perhaps it was Mozart whom she listened to all the time or maybe the Meadows itself. Adapting to the new doesn't come easily even though Karina should be used to it by now and the time to surrender to it was now. It comes when one least expects it or maybe when one wishes it strongly enough. It's a connection one makes with feelings of our past or a desire or just a hazy memory. Once revived one falls in love in this balancing act of different cultures and belief systems.

Karina was hoping for a cross pollination as they all swapped ideas making it able to join forces. Not all transplants saw eye to eye and Karina found herself being looked at as a hundred year old ruin talking nonsense as the Oracle of Delphi telling one's destiny. There was a pervasive mix of spiritual and sensual or just a religious mixing of civilization past and present, or was it a revisiting of tradition right out of the proverbial box?

The population bordered into worldly urbanite and laid back middle class. A mix of high and low, makeshift art galleries and artists'etaliers as well as run-down shacks and crystal shops. A lot of cultural activities for such a small community; she needed to try harder.

Just as the morning breeze shook the windows of her bedroom, the telephone rang. She barely heard it and yawning she answered:

"Hello, Good morning"

"Natalie this is Ann Phillips. I got your phone from Alice. I just found out that your last name is Sheffield. I knew a Sheffield a long time ago in London and am curious to know if you are any relation to him."

Karina totally woke up and sat straight up in bed. 'This is a dream' she told herself.

"Yes, I married a Glen Sheffield but I was known as Bravo, my first husband's last name."

There was total silence on the other side of the line.

"Karina, I am Ana Mendez. I don't want anyone to know about me. I was afraid that sooner or later Alice would put us together and figure out our connection."

"Oh, Ana you're alive. We have to tell Melina. We definitely have to talk. We looked for you for years and finally gave up believing that maybe you were dead, I am divorced from Glen. Can we meet as soon as possible?"

"This afternoon would be possible for me." Ana said hurriedly.

"Would you like to come over here? We would have all the privacy in the world and can talk to our hearts content."

"That sounds good. Give me directions. 2:00 Pm?"

"I'll be looking forward to seeing you again."

Karina got out of bed and ran to take a shower so she could be ready and be able to call Melina before Ana arrived.

Ana was very frightened with such heaviness that she could hardly breathe. She didn't know if she could face the past without hurting Karina. All the love, hurt, anger were crawling through her body as if an insect had invaded her veins. Deep inside she knew this day would come and she was glad to see Karina. Could it be like old times?

The temperature had stayed at 70 degrees with a hint of rain and a gentle breeze blowing the leaves. It was an ideal twilight tinted with a background of lavender flowers and scent. Ana felt relieved and glad to have found her friends and being able to bring all in the open.

"We have to call Melina." Ana said in an imploring voice.

"I already called her and gave her the good news. She wants to have a three way conversation, she doesn't want to miss anything and even suggested flying over here. It's been a long time!!!!!"

"I am so sorry that I disappeared like I did but I had no choice and I hope you can both forgive me." Ana covered her face as if about to cry.

The rush of emotions surrounding Ana's reappearance roared in like a tropical storm. They both were happy and in great expectancy of the meeting scheduled.

Karina called Melina to inform her of the details and the conversation to be held next day at 2:00

"I'll call you and we can have a three line conversation or at least speaker telephone. Wish you were here. Hard to believe how this has turned out"

"Keep me posted and please call, I want to hear her voice."

"Stay around in the afternoon, my time. I am so excited that I can hardly stay put. I think I will go for a long walk. Relax, tomorrow will mark history for us. Love you."

Police Report

A Mercury Way resident came to the station to report a theft. She said she and her husband got into a fight the previous night over money. They went to bed and when she woke up, she found her husband gone. She advised he took her purse, all her money and her car. She was advised to get a lawyer since this was a civil matter.

Chapter 20

An older, high voltage woman kept looking intensely at Karina. Outside of the salt and pepper hair and a very thin body, Ana looked exactly the same.

Looking at Karina, Ana feared the worst and reluctantly prepared to face her past. All of a sudden the world appeared strange and full of transformative events, questionable at their best.

Ana had loved Karina. The times spent in Spain were magic, exciting, mixed with tension, apprehension and even fear but being together fighting for the same goal made it all worthwhile. Now here she was facing the unpredictable but full of relieve knowing that she did not have to preoccupy herself anymore with what she had run from for so long.

Karina had prepared some pinas coladas like old times. She turned on the fire in the fireplace for a cozy atmosphere. After all the hugging, Karina spoke first.

"I am here all by myself. The children are married and living their own, great lives. I have three grandchildren and one on the way. I try to see them at least once a year. I married and divorced Glen Sheffield, he betrayed me with my own sister. I have felt kind of naked but trying to make a life here and so far, I think I have left my pain, fear and sadness behind. Instead a sense of belonging is trying to make its way through. I don't feel like a foreigner anymore."

Melina interrupted:

"You are a universal being, Karina. I stay a foreigner in my adopted land."

"Did you marry Carlos?" Ana inserted.

"Yes, and I have two lovely demons. I am very happy and complete but let's hear about you. Start with the visit to Paris."

Ana took a deep breath, swallowed hard and prepared herself to open that fateful door for good or bad.

"Paul picked me up at the airport and drove to his hotel. I was totally overwhelmed by the scenery shifting past us as he sped through the busy highway full of street lamps lighting the many shops—designers clothes, shoes, bags, perfumes. Many people hurried from shop to shop while couples kissed and held hands. Romance was in the air."

"Do you find Paris as romantic as it is known for?" I inquired.

"Oh, my goodness yes, it feels as if one should be in love, it is demanded". Paul answered laughingly.

"I am going to have to go to a meeting so I'll drop you off and let you settle in. I will be back around five to take you to dinner."

"That sounds great! I'll go for a walk. I need to stretch my legs and the area looks like a painted canvas so I think I'll enjoy it very much."

"Just be careful, especially of crazy drivers."

We passed the Champ Elysees with its many well-known shops. At the foot of the avenue Paul pointed to the Place de la Concorde:

"If you don't behave I can bring you here to cut your head off—it's the site of the infamous guillotine."

"I'll remember that and make sure to watch my P's and Q's"

"If you want to spend all your money here is the avenue Montaigne home to Chanel, Dior, Givenchy.

Here is the avenue de l'a opera and our hotel, you are surrounded by the best of Paris, my cherie."

"I was totally impressed with it all and Paul was just divine.

He kissed me after helping with my suitcases and left for his meeting. I was about to change clothes to go for my walk when the doorbell rang. I answered and to my surprise, a couple stood in front of me. They said they needed to talk to me before Paul got back. It was very important. I let them in."

Tears dropped from Ana's eyes, the episode became so vivid as if it was right in front of her.

"Ana, Paul is very sick. He is incurring into a lot of expenses. His insurance is demanding that in order to pay he had to have lived with someone that has cared for him for at least a year. You are the only person he sees and although you do not live together, the little white lie will help him so very much to no trouble to you. I am Nellie Travis and this is Glen. We are close friends of Paul's."

I felt awful. Paul had not mentioned anything to me and was somewhat apprehensive although I did not question his own brother's ill doing.

I would like to talk to Paul about it."

"You can't, he will never allow it. I can handle it without his ever knowing what has happened and maybe later you can both laugh about it."

Explained Nellie.

So I signed the paper, they left and I went for my walk. I was so sure I had done the right thing. I liked Paul too much, I probably loved him.

"Did you read any of what you signed?", asked Karina.

"No, Nellie gave me a very legal paper that said I would not be responsible for any damages. I believed her."

"Do you have a copy of that paper?" Melina was very nervous.

"Nellie said she would send copies in the mail. She had to process the whole thing fast so that Paul's next treatment would be covered."

"Did they tell you what was wrong with Paul?" Melina interrupted.

"Something to do with his blood. He was a hemophiliac. I was so non informed, I didn't want to sound like so. I had known Paul for over a year!"

"Well, the whole thing kept pounding my head and I was trying to figure out how to ask Paul about this illness of his. All of a sudden this car came at me, hit me and I was thrown down a cliff. I remembered it was a jaguar but could not see the driver. I woke up at the hospital but couldn't remember what had happened. I think I kept coming in and out of my comma because I remember when Nellie came into the room and introduced herself as Daniela Cortes to the doctor, and claiming me as her only relative.

I became very scared for some reason and left leaving a note on the mirror C A T. hoping someone would put all together. Again I ended up in this new hospital where I met Ron. I didn't remember much except that Karina, my good friend had a sister named Daniela.

Ron was doing a study in England and sat with us in our panel discussions. I went through analysis for five years. The period became a wake-up call where I started to appreciate this stranger that was me as I got to know myself more and more. Ron huddled closer and closer as we thumbed through the pages of what I could put together. I was confused with an occasional numbness. These symptoms came and went. Everyday brought more revelations and while finding myself, we fell in love."

"Can you get me more Pina colada, please."

"Certainly. Ana, during all this time you never thought of us or Paul?" Melina had trouble asking.

"I had flashes of you and Paul but couldn't put it all together.

We got married and settled in London. We wanted to stay in Europe and bring up the children there. The children grew up, made their own lives and Ronald was offered a position at the local hospital here and we moved to the Meadows. I left my comfort zone to follow my husband. With two mortgage payments, one in London and one in the Meadows, the situation was needless to say scary. Having gone through all the pain, running, hiding, I had faith in my inner voice. It wasn't long when the house in London sold and harmony was restored.

At least the financial worries were over. In a couple of years Ron's business expanded and we started enjoying life in the Meadows. I have been remembering more and more but afraid that something will show up one day and force us to face a legal matter. I think that your sister Daniela was driving the car that hit me but I am not sure. I am sorry Karina, I wouldn't want to hurt you for anything in the world and that's why I did not get in touch."

"Don't worry I parted company with my sister. I would not allow her to hurt me anymore, The karma is settled. If she has done this to you she should pay for it. She must have known Glen from way back. They used me."

"Where does this lead us?" Melina wanted to do something and fast.

"I don't know. We need to discuss it thoroughly and decide if we want to go to the police. Do we want to tell Paul?" Karina sounded concerned.

"I don't know that Ron would want to bring all up again. We have to discuss it with him. Your dear sister knew Glen a long time before you did. She had been in Florida a long time before she called you. I just have bits and pieces from my family mostly, who found out that she had left shortly after we did. Also from them that she lived with the family of an insurance agent and she had become a legal secretary. Ron and I figured that she met Glen through the family she lived with but this is not for sure."

"But why? What was the purpose of it all?" Melina could not understand the plot.

"We think they all worked together cheating the insurance companies."

"Where do I come in? What was Glenn's plan?" Karina was about to start crying.

"We think he did not count on falling in love. By then Daniela started blackmailing him. I am just trying to put together what happened and what the police has found out." Ana tried to explain.

I think I am going to make plans to come over. I want to see you and I certainly want to know everything. I am so glad you are alive and with us again. I love you."

Melina sounded off.

"I have to go too. We are going to New York mixing business and pleasure and I have to get ready. Thank you. I feel better about it all. I am so glad I found you. We will talk when I get back, in the meantime give it all a good thought. Let's see what we can come up with. I am starting to see a light at the end of this tunnel."

Karina hugged and kissed Ana and promised to give all a thought and have something in mind when she got back from her trip.

Pretty exhausted, she went to bed and cried herself to sleep.

Karina could not believe all that had happened and worried about what was still to come. She drove to work planning and trying to put together all that she knew till now. On arrival at the hospital, she met with Audrey looking wonderful. She was slim, picture perfect, bright eyed. Apparently a very happy woman. Karina had not seen or heard from her in two years and here she was full of hopes and expectations. She was still seeing Karl.

"Oh, Karina he is so good to me and the kids! The sex is the best I've ever known. He has introduced me to ways to obtain pleasure that you can not imagine! We can't have enough of each other!"

"Good for you but it always amazes me when people talk about the immense pleasures of sex. I am curious—tell me one thing you do different that brings this on"

"Oh, for one, he wants me to always wear a loose shirt with no underwear. This way I'm always accessible to all kinds of caresses, touching, poking. It makes it easy since the kids are always around. Sometimes a quickie which is always very welcome."

"I would think the kids are being exposed to a very dangerous situation. They are at that age, Audrey"

"We are in love and they know it."

"Be careful and I'm glad things are working out for you."

Karina knew that there was no point in going any further. Audrey was where she wanted to be.

She went home shaking her head in disbelief.

Police Report

"It's my fault, I ran the stop sign!" A maroon Nissan went airborne, landing on a Ford after running the stop sign on Saturn Rd. and Milky Way Blvd. John Roberts was injured and air-lifted to the hospital.

Chapter 21

Karina stayed in a dazed state for a long time. She tried to make sense of Ana's story. Daniela attempted murder? Was she having an affair with Glen? Were they using her? Should she call the police, Glen?. Did she want to stir up a bad nightmare?

She served herself a cup of tea and went to bed. She tossed and turned but finally fell into a deep sleep.

The morning came faster than she expected being a weekend when she usually slept late. She served herself a glass of vegetable juice and a cup of coffee. She proceeded to muddle the whole drama. She needed to talk so she dialed Melina who was about to call her.

"Give me your thoughts on what has happened." Karina asked Melina.

"A lot doesn't make sense and yet knowing your sister, it could all be a HORRID PLAN GONE BAD. For one, I got in touch with Paul and he said he is not sick, never hemophilia. He doesn't think Glen is part of it. He never met Daniela. He is so glad that Ana is safe and alive. He thinks we should notify the police and Interpol in London."

"We want to do the same but Ana wants to discuss it with Ron. I am afraid for myself and my family and of course Daniela's part in it."

Karina started to sound mentally disturbed.

"Hey, You must not come to conclusions without proof.

I am planning on coming over right after Thanksgiving and before Christmas. Carlos is taking time out to look after the boys. I can hardly wait. I'll talk to you soon."

Melina was reassuring and Karina could pick it up.

"Right kiddo! I love you."

Karina decided to go for a walk to clear her head if that was possible. She was at the door when the telephone rang.

"Hi, Barbara here. Jessica has invited everyone on the street for dinner to meet her new man David"

"Oh, Barbara I'm sick of this game Jessica is playing. I don't think I want to attend."

"It's a free dinner and you have to admit she puts on a good spread. It will get your mind off what it is that has been bothering you and which you haven't shared with this your friend."

Karina ignored the comment.

"I'm on my way out the door. Let me see how I feel when I get back from my walk Ok? I'll call you."

Karina could smell the pine needles falling as well as the acorns from the oaks. The wind was cool and carelessly blew her hair off her face. She sped her walk to the feel of the breeze that she so much liked. She got a sense of herself and how much she had accomplished. She was not going to let Daniela to take this away from her. She decided to call Glen as soon as possible. After walking an hour she returned home invigorated with strength to meet the inevitable.

"Barbara, I'll join you to have dinner with Miss Jessica and her new beau. I hope this one is not dead by the end of the year. I have to shower and get ready. See ya."

Not many residents attended the party. There were only six of them. Everyone expressed their excuses and were not coming. Jessica took it with a grain of salt. She really didn't care. The new man was very sociable and attentive and looked smitten with her. She did have a way with men. Karina left early almost right after dinner and Barbara immediately followed.

Tired but happy that she had decided on something, in this case calling Glen. She went to sleep as she reassured herself that all would work out for the best.

The ring of the telephone made a long, deep cut in her sleep. Dusk still covered the bedroom. She finds the monster and pushes talk. The November sky has turned light blue and the wind whips over the drying straw colored hills through the opened window, Karina rubs her eyes to bring herself back from Morpheus arms.

"Hey, girl, it's ten o'clock!. We need your presence. Can you sub?"

Karina laughingly answered;

'Wha ah nevaaaahh!!" In perfect southern accent.

"I do declare!"

"Oh Karina you can come up with the funniest outbursts!"

"I structured today as a day of indulgence, relaxed lunch, shopping but I can squeeze you in always for Bridge. I'll be there."

Toying with the fruit on her plate, she looked at the newspaper, sipped her coffee and her thoughts drifted to Ana. She could hardly wait for her to come back so they could resolve the situation, an uncomfortable one indeed. She added some sweetener to her coffee. It was a perfect cup now and her taste buds purred as she walked to her bedroom to get ready for the day.

She stopped at the mall to pick up a couple of gifts for the grandchildren. They always expected something from Grandma. She found the perfect things she wanted and was very pleased with herself. She found a cashmere sweater she had always wanted and bought it for a fantastic bargain. For a moment Glen stood next to her smiling as she recalled London and her visit to Harrods'.

After a lemonade and a delicious flounder, she went to her Bridge game and possibly the best gossip available.

"HI YOU ALL"

"You're just in time to hear the latest."

Mary Ann could barely wait for Karina to sit down.

"Remember Louise who has married 5 times or something like that? She's been with 5 men anyway.

Well, she had to call 911 because her latest died while having intercourse. He had a heart attack. I understand she was hysterical as the paramedics pulled him out from her."

"Oh, how awful!

I suppose that will be it for her. I would be so embarrassed I would move.

Of course I would not be doing what she is doing, not because I am judgmental but because it is so demeaning!"

Karina felt insulted.

"I don't know, I bet she will go right back to her business. Well, let's play."

The evening went by very fast and they played until midnight, Karina loved the game and hardly noticed the time. They played the last rubber and all went home not before scheduling the next month to play. They all teased Karina for making that fantastic grand slam.

"When are you leaving for Thanksgiving?"

Barbara asked Karina as she yawned.

"I'm leaving Saturday and will stay until the following Sunday. I am really looking forward to it. When I come back, a friend of mine from Spain is coming to visit and soon after I'll explain all the happenings going on in my life right now. I am not excluding you, you just will not understand. When I resolve the situation, I'll be able to let you in on it. I don't understand it myself right now."

"It sounds like a mystery movie. I know you will tell me when the time is right. Need a ride to the airport?"

"Yes, I do. I'll call you tomorrow and give you the details."

Arriving at Karina's house, Barbara kissed her goodnight promising to be there for her if she needed her.

The Meadows emptied for the holidays. Those who stayed, had their families over for the celebration but most left on a trip, cruise or visit relatives. It was like a written code. All activities ceased until whatever holiday was over.

Thanksgiving was wonderful and unforgettable. The food was a gourmet dream come true since both Nicolas and Karen enjoyed cooking. Adriana informed them that her husband had been offered a job at a local hospital in Houston, TX and the offer was too lucrative to pass up.

"After all the care and effort I put on our home in CA, we have to start all over again."

Her husband came over and hugging her said:

"You will also live closer to your mother, pay no state taxes and have more money to spend."

"I know, and closer to Nicolas too. I am really excited, sweetheart, and besides, it's a great recognition for you."

"Congratulations are in order. Let's toast to that and I am delighted" kind of sang Karina.

The kids had invited a retired doctor—a surgeon who had lost his wife three years back. He lived next door when he was in town. He spent his time helping people who needed some kind of surgery in different nations of the world . . . Karina was very impressed with his work and the way he thought. Something that Karina would not mind doing at all if she could stop working to make money.

Morgan Davies was in his late 60's, nice clean features pronounced the wrinkles earned from living to the most. He had no children and he wanted to travel but not to just go to be able to say that he had seen Belgium on his way to Germany. He wanted to be of service, so he joined Doctors without Borders and had been so very satisfied and content for having chosen to help others as he got to know their culture and lifestyle.

Karina understood perfectly because she never felt so satisfied in a job as she was working at the hospital. Morgan joined in the fun, walks and dinner with the family and fitted in as if he had been part of the family forever. He and Karina promised to stay in touch and he would visit her in the Meadows, right now he was getting ready to go to South America.

Thanksgiving over, Karina returned to her home and work. She had to get ready for Melina's visit. It was always hard to say goodbye to the children and grandchildren. Someday, maybe, hopefully, she could be near them, right now she had to continue earning her income to support herself.

Meeting Morgan was very refreshing and he made her feel very comfortable. She could easily imagined what he was feeling and why he was doing it. It was truly satisfaction guaranteed and she was somewhat overwhelmed by this man who seemed so detached from the world and yet so intensely involved. Karina was very attracted to Morgan. Yes, indeed.

Arriving at her home Morgan had left a message on her machine asking her to call him anytime, not to ever feel alone. Karina was touched: "maybe I can get to like this man, just maybe."

Would she be able to love again? Or even give of herself? The wounds left by Glen's betrayal and the hurt caused by her own sister were still healing and scars were forming but she did not want them opened again.

She would put this on hold until she resolved the mystery of Ana and Daniela. This pressed heavy on her shoulders and she needed to get to the bottom of it. Karina knew what her sister was capable of but this is murder, possibly, and she had to protect her family. How far would Daniela go to protect herself? Would she go after her children?. Karina had been reluctant to say anything to her kids for fear of upsetting them unnecessarily. No, it was better that she cleared up the experience with Ana. First things first.

Police Report

The police were summoned to the house of William Dewey where they found him dead on the kitchen floor. When he didn't show up for their date, nor answered the telephone, his girl-friend came over to check on him. Apparently his next door neighbor had killed him. Investigation is in the process.

Chapter 22

Ann had insisted on picking up Melina so she could have time alone with her. She had the jitters as she moved through the airport crowded aisles. Melina finally arrived showing the beautiful smile that so grabbed Carlos heart. Ann rushed into her arms and they hugged and kissed. They pulled away from each other and hugged some more. They looked at each other overwhelmed by the experience, one that neither imagined possible. The initial excitement gone, they started talking at the same time, asking questions and thanking the providence for their meeting. They walked hand in hand toward baggage pick up and customs.

"Are you happy with Carlos, Melina? Do you enjoy living in Europe?"

Ann anxiously asked.

"In those early years while we were dating and were lovers, sleeping carelessly on the beach, drinking wine and eating cheese and bread, it was intoxicating. We wandered around the streets of Barcelona as if we owned the world and I was seduced by the passionate moments that we shared while alone enjoying the sunsets. Life in Europe is good, relaxed with incredible sights and history so very good for Carlos to get inspired and write. Now it is busy but still we love it. I am in for whatever the ride offers. What about you? Did you fall in love with Ron right away?"

"No, Ron was sheer luck for me. I felt like I had lost my mooring and was kind of sinking and he rescued me. At the beginning it was gratefulness but it developed into love very fast. I've worked hard to get to a place of accepting what had happened. I voice my needs and we trade concessions making sure we express our gratitude for whatever we do for each other."

"You must have had a couple of hours of consciousness to be able to get out of the hospital by yourself."

Melina was jumping from one subject to another. There was so much she wanted to understand.

"In those moments of shock and horror that followed, I was numb. It all happened so fast. I could barely move and was acting, I believe, on instinct alone. You know the rest. Daniela is a bad person and I am still scared that she could harm my children. Ron is reluctant to stir all this, he doesn't think there is anything to be gained by it and could cause a lot of problems."

"I know, my dear, but we need to give it closure and to do that we have to face it. Karina, for example is harboring a lot of guilt and pain even though she claims she is fine. We need to discuss it with all around especially Ron.

Daniela has caused a lot of tears to Karina, she needs to find out the truth."

Ann took a sharp turn into the next street and Karina's house.

"Here we are."

Melina is totally impressed with the layout of the Meadows, not to mention what it has to offer.

"It's like a small town full of everything one needs to entertain oneself. It's like dream-land and so very peaceful and beautiful!"

"That it is" commented Karina with a bit of sarcasm in her voice.

They hugged and kissed. It was so unbelievable that they were all together again.

Melina looked great and immediately pulled the pictures of the children and so did Ann and Karina. They started sharing stories about them as they reminisce about Karina's children in Barcelona and how they never dreamed of this moment where the three of them had lived such interesting lives and had lived to discuss it. Little did they know when they left Isla Bonita that life would throw them such a curve. They laughed and cried and for now they were going to forget about Daniela.

Karina had prepared rice and beans and empanadas. As a touch, she fried some dwarf bananas to munch on. Sangria was a must and avocadoes for salad. A very typical Spanish dinner. The bread soaked in olive oil and balsamic vinegar with garlic, salt and pepper was gone as fast as Karina brought it out.

"Oh, wow, am I going to gain some weight, not that I care!"

Laughed Melina as she took a bite of a fried banana.

"Remember when we ate bread like this with a piece of cheese to save money for records? We gave the kids apples to make a complete meal."

"We drank lots of water to fill up as the record player kept repeating: the verb to be is the basis of the English language and must be understood before you get a hold of it. I am, you are, he/she is and on and on."

"Oh but we were so happy and so goal oriented. We just took a couple of weird turns while trying to get "there"

Dinner over, they moved to the kitchen to help Karina clean up. She put the dessert together, sopa borracha (drunken soup= a sponge cake soaked in rum) and some coffee. Each picked up their plate and moved to the den.

"Girls, I took the liberty to call Glen and he is claiming innocence but willing to meet with us. What do you say?"

Karina sheepishly notified them.

"I decided to talk to Ron about it and yes, get some closure. I will let you know what he says."

Ann sounded relieved.

Melina started applauding.

"Great, now we are getting somewhere. By the way Kari, this is superb!

I'll have another piece, please."

"You can have all you want. I'll wrap some for you, Ann to take home to Ron. It might sweeten him up for your conversation."

"I better get going, it's eleven o'clock and Ron will start to get worried very soon. I'll be here at 9:00 A.M. for the tour and more talking. I wish I could stay. Don't discuss anything new in my absence."

Ann kissed Melina and Karina good night.

Autumn was showing signs of moving on. The driveway was full of leaves and acorns. A cold blast of the upcoming winter air hit her face as she walked out the front door and she almost slipped on the pine needles covering the walkway. Ann buttoned up her coat and steadily and carefully entered her car and drove away. Her head couldn't handle any more information nor remembrance. It felt like it was going to explode. She had to put together how she was going to approach Ron and she needed a clear head for that. She slowed down to have time to sort it all. It was good to see Melina and glad she found Karina, now she had to approach Ron and the coming winter with confidence and aplomb. She smiled as if she had resolved the world crisis and sped home. She yearned for the security of Ron's arms around her.

Ron was up waiting for her.

"Did you reminisce enough?" Come here, you look tired and cold."

Ron extended his arms for her and she graciously fell into them.

"That's exactly what I was yearning for." Ron, the girls and I feel that we should resolve the hit and run incident once and for all. We need to put closure on this part of our lives especially for Karina"

"I was always leery of this day but I knew it had to come. Yes, let's get it over with. What are the plans? because I'm sure you have already started on something."

"You know what, I love you so very much! Let's go to bed and I'll tell you all about it tomorrow."

Ron guided her to bed where they snuggled under the comforter after kissing each other good night.

Police Report

A woman and her significant other called the police because of threatening calls from their ex-partners. On arrival the police found the man passed out on the kitchen floor. After some interrogation it was found out that the woman was having an affair with the next door neighbor who had come over and angrily hit the man. The case is under investigation.

Chapter 23

The crisp air beckoned Karina to start looking for warmer clothes and a good book to cozy up in front of the fireplace.

For Karina the chill banished counting sheep and she enjoyed countless hours of blissful sleep. She has never had problems throwing herself in bed and falling asleep but winters made it so much easier, faster to drift away to the wonderful land of Nod.

In the mornings, sitting in the porch with a cup of coffee, one could catch sight of a flurry of falling leaves shaken by the cold breezes. One can immediately want to cuddle up in one's favorite blanket. Pretty soon the ground will be covered with acorns and pinecones wet with rain and somehow with the change of the season, the urge to start thinking Christmas is to follow. With all that is happening, Karina doesn't have the same feelings for decorating or even celebrating. This year she was going to stick to the serenity and simplicity of white. An all white tree brought a quest for reflection and a winter nirvana. She was even buying white pajamas for herself and everyone on her list.

Karina felt the effects of all her thoughts and she was summoned to get something warm and hearty. She dropped the blanket that was keeping her warm and walked to the kitchen for a cup of hot coffee. She felt very invigorated and decided for a piece of pastry—yes, a piece of coffee cake that she had made for Melina the night before. She decided to write down the recipe for Southern corn while waiting for her to get up and which she wanted.

Karina had taken a week off from work to entertain Melina and plan a course of action to resolve the hit and run event. Today she was having them all for an early dinner to discuss feelings and how to proceed. Much has happened and much water has passed under Daniela's bridge to drain a team of mules. Karina was to either win the respect of her family and friends or be mocked for ever and ever. It was her responsibility to get to the truth and have justice take its course. Glen was coming and that made her uneasy. The day was cold and lazy with a breeze blowing the trees and mingling with the sounds of music from the record player echoing rhythms through the pristine meadows.

Melina left a sorry backdrop of memories gone by and a plan to be put in effect right away. Something like 'let's get it over with'. Some serious work was about to start and Karina wanted it all worked out by the Spring. She turned to face Melina who was trying to open her eyes.

"I think I overslept but ohhhhh, so good. I can get used to this life very quickly. So peaceful, quiet, undisturbed"

"Come on in and join me with a cup of coffee. I was writing the corn recipe you wanted."

Oh, yes, thanks, that was yummy. So very different."

"It's very Southern. Karina do you think you can handle whatever we find about Daniela?"

"I think I am prepared for the worst. Serve yourself some coffee cake. Want some eggs? There is a bowl of fruit."

"Fruit and the coffee cake sounds perfect."

"Glen will be here at 1:00 P.M. I asked Ann to be here at 3:00 P.M. Are you ready for all this?"

"As ready as I will ever be. Did Glen give you any trouble when you asked him to come?"

"No, he wants to clear his name of any wrong-doing. He claims he didn't know Daniela until she showed up at our house."

"Interesting. Hope he and Ann's stories match."

"I do too"

They both left to get ready for the fateful afternoon.

Glen was right on time. He was always very punctual. He looked a little misplaced and nervous but good-looking as ever even though he was losing his hair and had gained some weight. Karina greeted him politely but Melina hugged him apprehensively.

"Girls you both look exactly the same."

"You liar, we are old and pudgy."

"We all get that way at this age, but you are both gorgeous. You left Carlos all by himself? I am surprised he let you being the typical Spaniard that he is."

'Oh, no, he is very liberal, plus he knew how important this is to me."

"I am glad you called and are willing to hear my side of the story."

"Great, let's start from the beginning. When did you meet Daniela?"

"I met Nellie Travis in Florida when she started dating my friend John Miller. John and I were in the insurance business together after meeting at a convention in the Keys. I left Florida after marrying Lynne and settled in Colorado but John and I stayed in touch.

Nellie and John became a twosome and moved in together a year after they met.

Nellie became very knowledgeable of the insurance business and rapidly learned the loop holes. She had no problem with twisting the law "a little bit."

I knew this and didn't approved but went along with it because of John. It was not hurting me anyway, it was their way!"

Nellie came up with the idea about the policy and Paul. I was having problems in my marriage. All the money really belonged to Lynne, so I listened. Paul was a prime subject for a viatical settlement. No one will get hurt and all will profit. John and Nellie were to divide the profits with me and all I had to do was to introduce Paul to Nellie. Nothing to lose and no one to know.

We flew to London and found out about Ana, and Nellie changed her mind. It was a better deal to have Ana sign a policy in Paul's behalf for $5,000,000, we backdate the policy and Ann disappears, we pronounce her dead and collect in Paul's name. A humanitarian investment to say the least because Paul uses the money to pay his horrid hospital bills. This would certainly enhance the quality of their relationship because Paul would be more relaxed and worry free. That is all I agreed to, I swear."

"You actually agreed to breaking the law just like that and put your own brother in danger, and what about poor Ann who was an innocent bystander?!"

"I was sure that they would not be hurt. Nellie and I left after getting Ann to sign the papers, she left me in our hotel and asked for my car to do a little shopping and get copies of all the paper work. I took a nap. That is all I knew. When I questioned her she said all had gone as planned and I did not see nor hear of her until Nellie showed up at our house as Daniela. What a shocker!"

"What did you do with the car?"

"Nellie insisted on taking it to the outskirts of London and had it traded. We did and I bought a Mercedes and returned to London. Nellie returned to

Florida. I met you. There was no connection between you and Nellie. I didn't even know you had a sister. I told John I wanted no part of the deal."

"Didn't you find it strange that Nellie wanted the car repaired?

"No, I thought that we should not leave any trace of our being there at Paul's."

"Didn't Paul call you and inform you about Ann's disappearance?"

"Yes, but I didn't know anything and didn't want to tell him about the policy because Paul was so straight!"

"You mean honest"

The door bell rang and Karina excused herself to get Ann.

Ann became a little dizzy when she saw Glen and Glen was very uncomfortable.

"I am so sorry if I caused you any harm."

"No, No harm, just a little memory loss, five years of therapy, the fear, anxiety, the pain of not knowing who I was, no, nothing big."

Ann was very sarcastic.

"It cost me my marriage and the woman I love" Glen replied almost in a plea.

"I don't want to talk to this person anymore, I am leaving"

With that said, Ann picked up her purse and was ready to leave when Melina took her aside as Karina asked Glen to leave.

"We will be in touch, thanks for your input."

"Well, what do you think?" It looks like something Daniela would do, and yet why did he have the affair?" Was he blackmailed by Daniela?"

"I think we should notify the police and let them handle the whole thing.

"I agree" injected Ann." I am not afraid anymore. I refuse to continue being the victim. We were used by these unscrupulous people and it is our fault because we were so unaware, we paid dearly for our ignorance and misplaced trust, so now let it be."

"Let's sit down and try to put what we have together and then call the police" suggested Melina.

"I'll go fix something to munch on" Karina added as she got up and walked to the kitchen.

It was a very strenuous afternoon but one which dispelled a lot of doubts and brought new found information. The three of them were pleased and ready to open the case if such was what was needed. Karina proceeded to serve lunch and go over the conversation.

"We have to write this down. What if Glen denies what he just told us?"

Ana was still shaking from the encounter. Melina started dancing around with a tape recorder in her hand and started flashing it back and forth.

"I taped everything, so do not despair."

"Melina you are God sent" Ana gave her a big hug. "Kari, this lunch is what my doctor ordered".

They reminisced some more on the good old times as they ate and drank the afternoon away. They were happy and satisfied with the outcome. Now they had to prepare to approach the police. Melina reminded them that she had to get back to her husband and kids but would be in touch by telephone. They all agreed that the worst was in the open and now it was up to what the police could do. Karina would keep her posted on the details of the case.

"Melina, I'll take you to the airport since Kari has to go to work. I'll be here at 8:00 sharp. Thanks, Kari for all your help, I'll call you tomorrow night. I am going home and take a long bath."

Ana got up and hugged both and headed for the door. It had been a long afternoon. As she drove home she felt the weight on her shoulders had diminished. She felt like a new woman.

Police Report

Officers responded to an alarming call at Orion Way. A woman said there was a young man in the street beating on someone with a heavy stick. The police found out it was a snake. The woman backed out of her garage into her driveway and hit the police car. She was cited for unsafe backing.

Chapter 24

In December, the Meadows shifts to a holiday mode with crisp weather, barren trees as residents leave and or make plans to be with their respective families. The cold days turn into brisk nights. Everyone bundles up in winter coats and sweaters but mostly sweat suits or casual flannel shirts. The aroma of roasted chestnuts permeate the air. Twinkling lights and Christmas decorations fill the streets and club's windows. A lot of the stores in the nearby town display assorted quilts, one favorite pastime of the residents.

Karina tried to realign her energies and prepare for the confrontation that she has tried to avoid for so long. All of a sudden she felt immensely powerful. She was hearing a silence and she settled into its stillness to plan her approach. She was hoping this would be the only encounter with the police. She would provide the information she had and they would resolve the whole mystery all by themselves.

"I don't know why all this happened, didn't expect it to happen and we don't know how it all happened."

She addressed the police with confidence and self-assurance. She was totally enrapt in this quest and she had lost track of time thinking vividly about the scattered memories of the events that took Ana away for so long.

As the sun kept setting throwing a warm feeling on the living room, the conversation started with Karina speaking.

"This situation happened in Paris, so I don't know how much you can do."

"We will get in touch with them. Just give us what you have."

Ana took over when she noticed Karina getting emotional.

"Is this Nellie your sister?"

The police was addressing Karina.

"Yes, but I don't know what name she goes by now or where she is"

"Her real name is Daniela Miller" injected Ana.

"We know about her and her relationship with Miller. Miller would like to find her also. Apparently she took off with a lot of millions and left him holding the bag of errors."

"So you have been looking into it!"

"Oh, yes and so is the Insurance company. Miller's company has been closed for a while even though he tried bankruptcy. A very dangerous girl, your sister."

Can we have the tape and all the information obtained from the conversation with Mr. Sheffield and Ann's version of it all?"

"Yes, we made a copy. You can have this one."

"Thank you ladies, we will be in touch."

Ann and Karina breathed a sign of relief and sat down to sip a cup of cocoa with cheddar cheese, Spanish style.

"I feel so relieved but embarrassed!" Karina whispered as if afraid to be heard.

"Maybe all will end well for everybody, I'm all for forgiveness" Ann replied with a whimper.

"Can you stay? With Melina gone I feel kind of lonely" Karina begged.

"Let me call Ron and tell him about how it went with the police and see how he feels about my staying at least for dinner."

"I'm putting all those left-overs together and make a great salad. He can join us if he wants." Karina moved to the kitchen while Ann made her call. The ring of the telephone interrupted her culinary endeavors.

"Mrs. Bravo, the young man who had the motorcycle accident has just died. We need you to notify his family and get their permission for organ donating."

The hospital's organ unit was very apologetic but they needed to get the organs as soon as possible. Karina of course, obliged. This was the part of her job that she did not enjoy but was so necessary. She asked for the information and telephone numbers and proceeded to take care of the matter. The mother agreed to donate all organs except his eyes not before taking her time to scream with the pain of losing her only son. Karina informed the agency and went back to take care of the problem with Daniela.

Ann informed her that Ron would join them, he was way too curious.

"Oh Kari I'll have a full night sleep with no turns and sweats."

Sang out Ann.

"I can allow my heart to heal, no more guilt."

Ron was not surprised of the outcome and very pleased that it was taking a turn for the better. The police apparently were on their toes and the fact that Nellie had double-crossed Miller was a plus on their side. There was no doubt that she did it all: we need to find her.

They moved to the kitchen to partake of Kari's masterpiece. They laughed at what had come out of all the leftovers. Ann pointed out to Ron that this dinner was a typical Barcelona experience.

She and Kari hugged each other over and over happy that they had found each other again.

Dinner over, reminiscing enjoyed, Ron and Ann left for their home.

Karina's days had taken the predictable routine. She missed Melina and a crescent of tears flowed down her cheeks. A sense of loss was felt as much as a relief of a welcome finality. She went to bed feeling so free.

She was about to fall asleep when the telephone rang.

"Karina I'm sorry to call you so late but Karl is trying to get in the apartment. We broke up and he can not accept it. He's kicking, screaming like a crazy man!"

"Audrey, call the police" Do it immediately. Call me tomorrow."

With no regrets Karina hung up and went to sleep.

Police Report

A Mercury Way woman said there was someone playing golf after hours. The visitor to the Meadows will not play after hours again and when he does play, he has to wear the proper attire and not his pajamas.

Chapter 25

Karina gave herself a nice, easy going week-end. After the turmoil of the police episode, she needed time to herself. She slept until 9:30 A.M. on Saturday and was still in a drugged state but in good spirits. She felt a big load taken off her shoulders. The police was in charge now and it was up to them to worry about what to do next. She felt she had done her part. She had to work on the feeling of embarrassment she had toward Daniela's behavior without mentioning the hurt that she caused to all involved. Hopefully the only thing left was to find Daniela and bring her to justice without too much damage done.

Winter provokes change in the trees and the birds, and as such, triggers on us an emotional response to change, to beginnings, to endings: a desire to settle in a preparation for holidays. It makes one peaceful. Cold weather and shorter daylight times tell plants and us, also to go slow, nap more. We tend to reminisce more and are more prone to forgive and forget, so memories become strong reminders of old loves.

This reminded Karina that she had to explain to Barbara what had been going on. She would give her a call on Sunday, she said to herself. She might have her over for lunch and then give her the long explanation of why she had been ignoring her. She served herself some cold cereal and another cup of coffee and proceeded to head for the porch. It was somewhat chilly but soon she would not be able to use it. The minute she sat down the telephone rang.

"Hi, Melina here, did you talk to the police? Anything new?"

Her melodic voice sounded disturbed but Karina ignored it.

"Not since the last time—nothing new. I don't think they will be in touch until they have something concrete to tell us"

Karina was about to say more when Melina interrupted with.

"Paul called to find out what had come of it all. The police got in touch with him. Of course he doesn't know any more than what he already declared. He was extremely surprised at the gall that this "Nellie" has. The police told him that she got the fake death certificate in Mexico. It is going to be difficult to find her because with that kind of money and the availability of plastic surgery, she could be somebody totally new by now. He feels bad for you and of course for Ann."

"Yes, it is all true. We have to wait and see. She has to make a mistake sometime. Everything ok with you?"

"Yes, getting ready for the Holidays. Carlos' book is ready for the press so we are excited. Call me if anything new happens and be careful!"

"Of course my dear. I'll keep you posted"

Karina went back to her now soggy cereal: she had taken two spoonfuls when the telephone rang again. She considered for a moment not answering it but then it could be the hospital. She swallowed the cereal still in her mouth.

"Hello!!!!!"

A very husky, virile voice came through and she straightened herself up waiting.

"Hi, I hope you remember me. This is Morgan. Morgan Davies."

Karina interrupted him. “Of course, how nice of you to call. Where are you?” Karina was trying to place him.

“Right here on your turf. I had to come to the hospital to give a talk. I won’t be here very long but wanted to touch base with you.”

All of a sudden the image of a tall, blue eyed, white haired man came to mind. She felt flattered. This easygoing, genuine, perceptive man with a great sense of humor remembered her.

“I am so glad you called. Do you have time to meet for a little bit?”

She was now hopeful and nervous.

“Yes, I have a whole day to myself and would love to share it with you.

Could you come to the Meadows?” Karina was testing the water.

“We could have something to eat here, talk and decide what to do with the little time that you have.”

“That sounds great. Give me directions, I can leave right now and we can have lunch together.”

Karina proceeded to give him directions to her house.

As soon as she hung up Karina started to get ready. She had gone through some terrible findings and her pain was not processing as fast as it used to. She kept going over and over all the information that she had gotten. How can anyone so close to her could have done something so unthinkable? She and Ann had struggled with all the happenings and the difference in which they grieved. Karina dressed simply, jeans and a blue sweater with boots. She kept going over her present feelings. She needed someone to help her take the pain away and here was this great man right at her doorstep. He could certainly free her of her shadows by getting her sense of humor to the forefront if nothing else.

The door opened to show the man that all of a sudden she remembered. Wisps of fog were sneaking in veiling the area with a mist and she was transfixed by the figure facing her. She let him in after giving him a welcome kiss on the cheek which he happily returned.

He explained the purpose of his visit to the area and the desire to see her again in hopes that they would continue the friendship.

"I like what I have seen, the Meadows is as beautiful as you described it. Can we take a walk?"

Karina could not ask for more. They took a meandering walk along the trail closest to Karina's house. It's a scenic walk with small water falls cascading along part of the trail. The cool air blows through the trees and Morgan puts his arms around her in a protective gesture. Karina had that butterfly feeling all over again. Her fears were obliterated by his nearness and she felt very comfortable. Holding his hand, the scenery became magical and they both valued the solitude attained. They walked back in silence.

Lunch turned into a discovery episode where each told each other their past experiences. Morgan thought the world of Karina's son and family and although he did not know her daughter very well, he really liked the way she was handling her life as the wife of a physician. As for Karina, she knew all about it since that was her life with Enrique.

"Would you consider joining us on a trip to Guatemala? We are going next month and could use an interpreter. All expenses will be paid and we can spend more time together. I would really like that."

"How long do I have to answer you?" Karina answered expectantly.

"Oh, five minutes." He joked.

"I need an answer within two weeks, I'm sorry but we need to get someone fast. Our regular is with her sick mother and can not attend."

“Just have to see how my schedule is at the hospital and will let you know. I think I will like that.”

“I’ll send you the details when I get back.”

Their lunch finished, they went to Karina’s house where they talked and laughed some more. Morgan explained to Karina what the trip entailed and the usual procedures. They were seeing the world from different angles. He inspired her and he felt so at ease in her presence. Their relationship could become soothing, reassured, making it a great friendship. Evening approached very fast and Morgan had to get back, he kissed her gently, softly and said goodbye.

“I’ll call you as soon as I get home and we will make plans. Take care and thanks for a lovely day”.

Karina hugged him feeling a sense of belonging that she had not felt since she had left her native land.

She proceeded to listen to her messages.

Audrey sounded desperate “I have to talk to you, please”

Karina called her right away.

“Let’s meet in the cafeteria tomorrow. I am very tired and need a goodnight sleep.”

“Can’t ask for more than that, thanks.”

Karina met a very different Audrey. She had lost her kids. Apparently her daughter Trish told her teacher about the fun they all were having at the apartment and the teacher called social services. Social Services showed up at the apartment finding Karl and Audrey walking around in their underwear.

"I don't want to see this man again. I want my kids back. I was told that their father had requested custody. Besides I found out that Karl had no money. His wife had left everything to her daughters, he only had the house they lived in. He lied to me."

"So you broke up with him over the social services episode or because he has no money. You are playing with fire."

"Right after that, but things had been getting out of hand. He became possessive and demanding and sex had lost its lure."

"So, where is he now, where are the children?"

"I'm alone. My ex took me to court and I lost custody of my kids. They are both with him and the witch. I am seeing someone else but Karl doesn't want to leave me alone."

"Hope you have learned your lesson and try to find a relationship based on values and for a starter get away from your mother, she is not a good influence."

"I know, I'm going to move out of the Meadows, get my own place and try to start over. You have been such a great friend. I hope we can stay in touch."

The next time Karina saw Audrey, she was helping her new husband in his business and had managed to get permission to see her kids. She seemed happy and so was Karina.

Police Report

The Meadows police seized a large amount of drugs and more than $10,000 in cash from an illegal drug dealer who fled by car and on foot before being apprehended Saturday evening. He has been living in the Meadows for two years. His house has been searched and closed for the time being.

Chapter 26

Karina was still in her nightgown sipping a cup of coffee in the porch when a fog rapidly descended transforming the Meadows into an eerie but gorgeous black and white setting. It was Winter alright offering a peaceful aura filled with defiance to make it to Christmas time without frustration, illness or sadness that old memories would bring.

The misty fog can hide a multitude of sins and Karina was hiding all her feelings behind a charade of busyness. It was a daunting task because she wouldn't be her up-front, honest self. She could always find some beauty, challenge or some reason to appreciate where she had gotten, which was now her home.

These mornings stole her breath as she realized she was just a shadow in this world that had become her refuge. She reached out for the telephone to call Barbara.

Hi! Will you be available for dinner? I want to bring you up abreast of events."

Karina sheepishly begged.

"I knew you would come around sooner or later. Of course I am free for you, plus curiosity is killing me."

Replied Barbara in a very happy tone.

"Come on over at about 4:00 and we can talk until we run out of saliva"

"I'll be there with bells on my shoes. Can I bring anything?"

"No, it will be simple."

Karina wanted to be still but she really wanted to jump up and shout out loud the relief that she felt going through her veins. She felt victorious and untouched by the time gone by. She had to control herself until the whole drama was resolved and that may take a long time.

"You are not the only one that is surprised."

Karina had just finished telling Barbara the story and Barbara was dumb founded. They finished dinner and moved to the den with glasses of wine that had been emptied twice by now.

"I hope you don't have to face your sister alone. You call me if she shows up."

Barbara was her helpful self.

"Oh no, I don't expect to see her unless we go to trial."

Tears came down Karina's cheeks. She was finally accepting her pain.

Barbara offered her some tissues and hugged her.

"Let's drop this sad story. I have to tell you about Morgan. He showed up here and we had a great time. I really enjoy him."

Excitement was in her voice and Barbara got excited with her. It was the first time that Karina showed any enthusiasm about a man.

"And, and? What now?" anxiously asked Barbara.

"Nothing, he left and will be in touch." It's very hard at this age to form tight relationships of any kind although I have to admit that if I were to consider a relationship, it would be with him. I don't know that I want to share my life with another man. I am very comfortable the way things are and I don't think I want to take care of anyone or plan dinners, oh Yak!"

"You'll change your mind as love takes over" Barbara teased her.

"Thanks, my friend, I am glad you are back into my life. I missed you. I'll call you, now I better let you get to bed since you have to work tomorrow."

They kissed each other goodnight.

Karina prepared for bed and as she went through the different moves, she decided to go to Guatemala with Morgan. She would have to notify the hospital and get ready. She picked up the telephone to notify Morgan about her decision. Morgan could not have been more pleased and informed her of the details with written directions to follow. They were leaving in two weeks. He also promised a call with more assurance. She went to bed and fell asleep immediately. She felt cuddled.

With the idea of the trip kicking in, Karina wipes her sleep from her eyes and gets dressed to hit the early morning, empty road to work. The chilly morning turns into a very cold, rainy drive into town. Sometimes she feels that she is doing everything backwards and it was going to be impossible to catch up but other times she felt so fulfilled that she thanked her lucky stars for this job. The drive was always relaxing and inspiring, kind of a timelessness that whispered to her of things to come or do. She always meditated all the way and she talked to the rocks as she drove by believing that she was helping the world to be a better place to live.

On arriving at the hospital, she found the staff up in arms. They were all young and their minds had not opened up to the reality of life.

"What's going on? Why are you so upset?" inquired Karina.

"Our health insurance has changed. Our premiums are going up and so is the deductible, we can't afford to get sick! Of course there are no raises."

Everyone is talking at the same time. Karina doesn't know what to say since she has a wonderful plan from her teaching retirement but joins the discussion to give them support. There is a full schedule for the day as Monday usually is. The secretary informs her that the girl scheduled to have her tubes tied has not responded to Karina's calls and her appointment is going to be cancelled and given to someone else.

Karina got on the telephone to phone her and on finding her, found out that she was already pregnant. Sometimes it was futile to try to help and she felt frustrated. She had to report to ER and proceeded to do so. Another accident at the saw mill had caused a girl to practically lose her arm. As Karina approached her, she whispered: "I think I'm pregnant, please take care of my baby."

Karina held her hand and promised she would notify the doctor. The girl was taken to surgery and Karina returned to her post. She is informed that Dr. Gaylord had announced his resignation as well as the new secretary and they were leaving for another hospital and another state and divorcing their respective mates. What a shocker this was to Karina!

She went to help her next patient and entered the room where she was with the nurse practitioner.

"I can't figure out what she is trying to tell me."

Karina addressed the patient in Spanish asking her to explain.

"My baby is not my husband's but his friend's. My husband is ok with that, better than from someone I picked up in the street. He was visiting waiting for my husband and we started to cuddle and before I knew it we were in bed doing it—a perfect shot because I got pregnant."

Karina translated for the nurse and they both shockingly said "OH, OK"

Later on they found out after the results from the tests came back that she had herpes. Now to find out who gave her the sexually transmitted dangerous, incurable disease. Karina would handle that tomorrow. Life was not dull at the clinic. She went home asking herself how in the world did these young girls made it in this world so foreign to them.

The trip to Guatemala was rapidly approaching and Karina had to get the necessary documents, vaccinations and paper work. She decided to devote tomorrow to this task and with no hesitation, informed the secretary that she would not be at work next day.

Police Report

A Pluto Lane woman called police to report that kids were playing on her roof. Then she called again to say that the mothers of the kids were up there also. She also explained that her chimney was wired so the kids could hear everything she said and asked the police to be careful because they would know that she had called them. On arrival, the police was notified that the kids had stolen her electricity. The police calmed her down and tried to contact a relative.

Chapter 27

Karina packed according to instructions given. "Nothing that you can not put in a back-pack". The whole team were staying at a small motel in Solala and walked to and from the clinic. Some days they could take the bus but this was not a certainty. She was to meet the group at the airport.

Barbara picked her up and after asking her to be careful a hundred times, left her standing like a poor orphan waiting for someone to take her home. She saw Morgan who waved and asked her to join them with a hand signal. They boarded the airplane with no difficulties and much apprehension on Karina's part.

Guatemala turned out to be a very colorful place with bougainvillea covering practically every building they saw. They took one of the "chicken buses" (old retired school buses shared by humans and animals especially chickens). Despite all the warnings of impending peril, the six hour trip into Lake Atitlan area was uneventful but impressive and picturesque. They went down curvy roads which made Karina extremely nervous. The crew had been here before and kept telling her details about Panajachel to keep her mind off the road. On arrival she found the whole Lake and surrounding towns and especially the three volcanoes spitting what looked like steam, magical. The Mayan culture was seen everywhere. Panajachel was at the bottom of the road, breathtakingly beautiful, providing a base for visitors to cross the lake to visit other towns and villages. It was going to be her home for the next ten days.

They unloaded the bags and equipment and Morgan pulled Karina aside. He emphasized the importance to facilitate the delivery of the best medical care based on need alone.

"You are here because I trust that you will be the perfect interpreter and conveyor of our mission statement. We will not be able to socialize much since your time is limited. It's a lot of work to be covered in a short time. Most of all I need for you to inform the patients of their treatment and document everything. Also you will be conducting evaluations to determine their medical needs and then get in touch with those communities that are not receiving aide and why."

"Do you want all in Spanish or English?"

Karina was amazed at his business like approach and knew that he was really devoted to his work and nothing was coming in his way.

"Both, if you please" was the answer in equal detachment.

"Are your accommodations adequate? Are they comfortable?"

"Yes, very. Thanks."

Karina was very polite and apparently that was the way to be.

She settled in her room which she was sharing with a nurse, Mary Lou.

"Do you want to take a look at the lake and maybe eat something? I'm starving" Mary Lou was being friendly.

"Sounds like a good plan" immediately answered Karina.

She finished unpacking, took a short shower and put on a blue sweat suit. They left to pursue this new adventure. The view was stunning and they walked to the nearest restaurant that looked more like a pub. Karina ordered some Spanish dishes that she had not tasted for years. She urged Mary Lou to try them and they both enjoyed their night out very much. With that done, they had a glass of wine and went back to get ready for next day's work.

"It will be very hard to leave this place."

The evening breeze swept into the room through the opened window and they fell asleep immediately.

A rooster woke them up way before the alarm.

"How quaint! What a nice way to face the day."

Mary Lou was totally taken aback.

"I am used to it and it is very nostalgic."

"Oh, that's right, you are originally from these suburbs."

"Not quite, but we share a lot of the same things" Karina answered with a mocking tone.

They boarded the bus to the clinic. It was certainly a full day as Karina tried to follow Dr. Davies' instructions to a T. The list was long and tedious as trying to get information from the patients to be was an act of strength. They didn't have the necessary information because they did not concern themselves with "Small" things like their birth date.

"We are born, we live the best way we can, we die and report to our creator of our deeds. It doesn't matter when we were born."

This was a local belief. They were happy people, contented with their lot and they had to be admired for that. Karina had found this at the clinic also.

Watching the lake with its majestic volcanoes wasn't something one did when time permitted: it's a must do ritual. When the sun begins to set, the brilliant colors intensify. It is a sight to behold.

Morgan had asked Karina to go for a sundown tour with him.

"You will experience a road of wonder as we walk down the boardwalk."

"Why a boardwalk? What is it?"

"So we don't step on the beautiful plants, as one gets carried away with the view that takes your breath away. How are you doing?"

"I'm enjoying every minute of it. No matter what I have to do, the calm and tranquility will have a lasting effect on me. What a gorgeous place this is."

"Let's go sip some coffee with a liqueur. Are you up to it?"

Morgan stretched his arm out to reach Karina's. He pulled her from the hammock putting his hands around her waist to guide her along.

"How so much like him. She doesn't hear from him for days and here he is, the epitome of charm." she said to herself.

“How are you liking it so far?” asked Morgan apprehensively.

“This has had an impact on me, seeing the locals ability to make do with essentially nothing and being so happy and thankful! And with it all my worries and concerns melt away. One kind of joins in giving me such a good feeling!. Thanks from bringing me here.”

“It’s my pleasure and I am the one that has to thank you for being such a help. Everyone loves you and is talking about how helpful you have been. By the way you did a grand job on the scheduling. Even after your departure, the clinic will be working up to par. We can make a great team, Karina.”

He brought her close to him and gave her a kiss on the hair. It was such a genuine gesture on his part and Karina’s stomach filled once again with butterflies. Like the proverbial martini he looked shaken but not stirred and she could not think about it too much.

Will all this be just a memory? This whole trip is turning out to be an idyllic escape.

They walked hand in hand back to the motel. He lightly kissed her good night. Karina pretended she was not trembling.

"Sleep well—It's going to be a busy day tomorrow. We are doing two very serious surgeries and I want you there."

"I'll be there and thanks, Morgan, for a lovely evening."

Breakfast was another culinary delight infused with local fruits and traditional dishes. This morning they were served corn meal with bacon and guavas.

Karina left for the clinic and the ladies in the kitchen promised a gaspacho for dinner (Codfish with vegetables) soaked in their own olive oil to be savored with their assortment of local vegetables.

The vibrant foliage beckoned the drive to the country side along the lake. The day was very busy with a leg amputation, surgery on a cleft lip, and two tubal ligations for which Karina had to get a church permit. She saw Morgan in passing by but was not able to say hi.

Karina tried to battle all the enchanted moments but how does one do that?

All the beautiful landscape, diverse languages and cultures as well as the typical cuisine demanded her attention and memory. The work that was being done was unparalleled to anything she had seen and Morgan was just a miracle.

That afternoon she opted for a massage and tea. She needed both. The massages were not luxurious but very relaxing and precise. Every single muscle in her body was accessed and worked on. She took a hot bath and put on a jogging suit and went to dinner. The delicious gaspacho set the tone for a very body, mind and spirit winding down. She went to sleep at nightfall.

Karina woke up again to the cock-a-doodle of the rooster outside her room. She got up and went to the outdoor patio which was facing the lake to greet the new day. She embraced the cool breezes and went in to dress. Emilia, the girl in charge of the kitchen, brought her a cup of coffee and a bowl of fruit. She took a sip of the coffee and a bite of a mango and rushed out to catch the bus. This was a typical morning during her stay except she tried different fruits.

Dr. Davies had already left as he is in constant state of efficiency. He uses every minute of the day productively as he is accepted and admired by everyone.

The whole week unfolded with easy certitude. She knew what to expect by now and she answered questions as a native. The routine was the same every day except on Thursday. Dr. Davies asked her to dinner in town.

They dined on a hearty stew, followed by empanadas (turnovers filled with meat). They sat at a table closed to the street to watch people go by. They sipped brandy with candied papayas with local white cheese. They walked back hand in hand.

"Karina, I really enjoy your company and can't thank you enough for joining us. You have been an angel."

"I enjoy yours also Dr. Davies. I want to check the chocolates and the butterfly sanctuary if time permits and then I leave. Time has flown by. I can see why you do this work and why you enjoy it so much."

"I have made it my life. I have a personal connection to all the patients I meet."

"I know, and it's very commendable. I admire you for it."

"Here we are, have some rest. I probably will not see you before you leave. You have been a saint, I wish you could join us but I will call you when I get back. Have a good trip."

He again kissed her on both cheeks, a hug and waved good night.

"This wonderful man was totally married to his profession."

She convinced herself that he could be the best friend any girl could ever have. Karina was not too sure that this trip had been good for her self-esteem. She went to sleep and woke up refresh for her trip back home.

Police Report

A Saturn Way man informed the police that he left at 10:am to get a birthday card for his granddaughter and upon returning, found his mail box in the driveway. Another nearby mailbox was also in a neighbor's driveway. The police is investigating.

Chapter 28

Karina had barely opened the door to her home in the Meadows when the telephone rang. She ran to answer it before the machine picked up.

"Mrs. Bravo, Lt. Reynolds here. I'm glad I caught you because we need to talk and fast."

"I am just walking in. I was in Central America."

"Well, welcome back. We think we know where your sister is."

Karina put her purse down and grabbed a chair for support.

"Where? Are you picking her up?"

"We don't want to scare her and have her disappear. She is actually in the U.S. In Arizona to be exact. Can we meet?"

"Yes, of course. Tomorrow at about ten o'clock?"

"Ask Ann to join us and I'll see you then in my office."

Karina took a hot bath to try to relax. The heaven she found in Guatemala was all of a sudden gone. Was is it ever going to end? She didn't know what to expect but that was the way it had always been with Daniela. She was tired and needed some sleep to face the new episode.

The leaves had blown off from the trees and small vestiges of snow dusted the area. The Meadows looked like a greeting card. The season of giving is here and Karina feels the pain and anger that Daniela is causing her doesn't let her welcome the season with the reverence and joy that she would like.

What she is to face swallows every sound of the Holidays and brings familiar haunts from the past. Reluctantly, she called Ann.

"Let me pick you up, you must be very tired from your trip not to mention the situation that we have to face." Ann offered although sadly.

"Thanks, my dear. At least we can see an end coming."

Lt. Reynolds introduced them to a gentleman, Henry Kent, who was representing the insurance company that Daniela supposedly stole from. He had been tracking every move she made since her apparent disappearance after collecting the money. He presented Karina with a picture.

"This is a picture of Doris Banks."

Karina looked at the picture and showed it to Ann. They looked at the pretty brunette without recognizing her.

"So, who is this?"

"That, my dear is your sister. She has been living in Arizona for the past ten years in a small town named Benson near Tucson, close to the border with Mexico where she had been before that. She's married to Anthony Banks, a real estate broker and owner of the largest agency in town. He has two children from a previous marriage, the marriage that according to the children, Daniela broke up. She had plastic surgery and assumed a new identity, met Tony who left his wife, married her and moved to this little town to start a new life.

Mr. Kent connected with the children who helped him get samples of her hair and a smeared goblet with her saliva and so identify her DNA. This helped him prove who she was. The children, also were able to find a key that turned out to be to a safety deposit box. With a police order, he was able to get into her safety deposit box where they found her passport, her birth certificate and part of the money stolen. She had pictures of you, Karina, your children and Glen which helped make the connection. This is the background on your sister. Now we need for you two to face her."

"I rather not do that".

Both Ann and Karina were reluctant to the meeting. The investigator explained the need to go to Tucson and testify if they wanted her punished for what she had done. Karina and Ann hugged each other and crying and sobbing accepted their lot.

"I have mixed feelings. I want her punished but I am also embarrassed and fearful. My sister can be very persuasive and dangerous and very believable too."

"I understand, and see where you are coming from. I hardly knew her and she turned my world around without notice." Henry Kent was trying his best to be persuasive.

"I know, and I am so very sorry" Karina said apologetically.

"OK girls, when can we take off for Tucson and get this over with? I do want to close this case also".

"I have to discuss it with my husband but can be as early as this week end."

"Same here." added Karina.

The meeting was not a pleasant one. John Miller was pacing the floor back and forth. Glen was looking very apprehensive, Ann was very scared and Karina terribly embarrassed and concerned for all. The whole scene had provoked a kind of insane happiness in Karina. So chilling was the whole event that she looked around for sudden changes but only witnessed a very defiant Daniela suggesting it was everyone's fault, not hers, and Karina, as usual was hurting her and disturbing her nicely planned life. Ann and Karina were really spooked and as such felt shielded and isolated from the life that Daniela created making them unwilling parts. Holding each other's hand, they took a breath of relief knowing that it would soon be over and eventually what had infested their souls would also heal. Daniela gave Karina a gesture with her finger as she was taken away.

All Karina wanted now was to crawl into bed with a fire going, look at the clouds in The Meadows crash into the Ozark mountains. She would close her eyes and be able to put the whole thing in the past and reunite with her life in the Meadows as she intended it to be with the grand bursts of nature surrounding her as she faced her retirement. She whispered to Ann:

"Let's get out of here, it's over."

"I'll be in touch if I need you. Probably just some paper work." The detective waved good bye.

Karina grabbed Ann's arm and they walked out not even saying goodbye to those present. There were no more doors, locks or even mirrors. All was simply resolved. Daniela was facing a few years in jail. The insurance agent smiled with satisfaction.

Ann and Karina boarded an airplane that same day for the Meadows. They barely talked on the way back, they were both exhausted. Tomorrow they had to call Melina or she would die of anguish.

The flight was easy since they slept all the way. Ronald was waiting for them at the airport. Arriving at her house, Karina kissed Ann good night and thanked Ronald. They agreed on meeting tomorrow and close the very sad chapter.

Karina did not hear from or about Daniela. She didn't ask about the trial or where she had been sent. It was better for her to pretend that Daniela had died, it was easier to accept.

Police Report

The police are checking the shooting of an elderly lady on Pluto Place after her husband called to inform them that he and his wife had an argument and he got mad and accidentally shot her. The lady is in critical condition at the local hospital.

Chapter 29

For weeks Karina did not feel like herself. Everyone used "that tone on her." She was afraid she was going to hit a depression stage. She didn't know what to do with her feelings of loss. She needed to get rid of the guilt and adjust to life without Daniela. She tried to tell Barbara about what had happened but instead a soft whimpering recounting the events came out of her mouth. The physical scars were also showing because of the lack of sleep and all the tension not knowing what to expect.

"Can't go on auto pilot, Karina, you have to be selfish and think of yourself."

Barbara's scolding tone was loud and clear.

"I know, intersected Karina, I feel guilty at times and then furious and today I feel just devastated because I have realized that I can't come to terms with my sister's behavior."

"It's too soon!. You have to build good memories with your kids and the people who truly love you. Replace the concerns over Daniela; you tried to help her, must break the connection, it's kind of a bad habit."

"You've been such a great support, Barbara. Let's get out of here and go for a café latte".

"That's my girl. Then let's go see a funny movie."

All of a sudden they both were in great spirits and sang all the way into town. The coffee hit the spot. Karina had emptied her concerns and the movie was very relaxing. They stopped for some prime rib that was served at their favorite restaurant and retired to bed early. Karina felt much better. They promised to call and talk later in the week.

Mother Nature is a fickle escort who gives only on its terms. This A.M. Karina woke up to a blanket of snow. Not having control of what is outside, she looked for warmer clothes to wear to work. It's not easy to look forward to the driving regardless of how fleeting it was.

There were a lot of cancellations and late arrivals at the clinic. Karina was to attend to a vaginal bleeding.

The patient, an eighteen year old female had vaginal bleeding last night and complained of "a white stuff" coming out of her vagina that looked like "fish bait". She also notified Karina that she had been assaulted. An ultrasound showed an intrauterine pregnancy. Karina notified Case Management for help on the assault.

After helping the nurse practitioner, she was summoned to the Medical office to help fill out an application. The patient is pregnant with her eighth child. Neither she nor boyfriend are working, she's also asking for food stamps. Karina notified her that the children had to have been born in the US to qualify for food stamps. She understood and would come back with all the necessary information.

"She should not have any more children" Karina was emphatic with her statement.

"I know but we can not urge them to do anything, it's against our rules. I took care of a girl on Friday who's in jail, pregnant. She doesn't even know who the father of the baby is. She hasn't brought the paper work, she smokes and drinks and we suspect she also takes drugs. Poor baby." expressed the Medicaid advisor as she shrugged her shoulders.

Karina's day went very fast. Her thoughts went back to the problem with Daniela. All the way back home she thought about getting her life back. It shouldn't be a mammoth effort, Daniela was gone and she had plenty of time to herself to create the wonderland that she deserved. She planned to achieve more balance and less inconsistencies, this is just "another pothole."

She was close to her quest and she would have to continue her journey and without worrying about Daniela. Driving back home she also thought about Morgan and how she wished it would be a different kind of relationship. But would she give up her freedom she had so enjoyed? Was she ready to share decisions that she has made by herself and what about planning menus? What about her children? Her life was so simple! Yet she missed the hugging and cuddling in the arms of a caring man. One can not have it all, she consoled herself, she better not even go there right now. The relationship was perfect as it was, no commitments and the pleasure of his company once in a while.

She opened the door to her house and the message machine was blinking with some messages. The dry cleaning was ready, the hospital wanted for her to call, Barbara needed her, Nicolas wanted to discuss something with her and then the telephone rang giving her a jolt. She answered it on the first ring. It was Morgan, he was going to be in town, could he see her. Why couldn't he say I'm coming to see you? It was always the by-product of some event. This did not help her insecurities.

Karina shrugged her shoulders in an effort to dismiss her fears. She answered in a very happy mood; "Hi, what a pleasant surprise! I was contemplating giving you a call."

"Why didn't you? You know my social life is always a last minute thing."

Morgan sounded a little apologetic.

"Our Christmas dance is in two weeks and I was hoping you could attend with me." It took all of Karina's courage to ask.

"That sounds wonderful—I love to dance and haven't done any of it in years. I'll be clumsy at the start."

"I'll accept that"

"It's a date. Is it formal?"

"Yes, but you can wear a dark suit."

"Does that mean we can spend Christmas together?"

Karina was taken by surprise.

I'm going to Adriana's new house. You know they moved to Texas. You're welcomed to join us" she said reluctantly—she really did not like to share these moments.

"Let me think about it but the dance is on, thanks. my dear. I'll call again for the details. Good night"

Karina kicked off her shoes, threw her purse on the chair in her bedroom and let a sigh of satisfaction and confusion but oh so content! She was smiling to herself when the telephone rang. It was Barbara.

"Hey, I kind of remembered that today you were going back to work. How did you fare?"

"Fine. I have to tell you I just finished talking to Morgan and you are not going to believe this but I invited him to the dance and he said yes."

"Great, we can sit together. I have reserved a table already. You are crazy for not making this relationship steady. I think he is waiting for you to make the move. We are not getting any younger and time goes very fast, my dear. He is better than most, what in the world do you want?"

"You are beginning to sound like the Meadows Singles Club women talking, desperate creatures afraid to let the love train go by."

"What do you rather want me to do? Play Chopin?"

"Barbara, stop. I really had a very nice day and I want to keep it that way. I don't know if I want to do what a relationship requires."

"Your life is not over, you are still writing pages to your life's history. Karina, you are probably the only person I know that still sends Christmas cards. Everyone e-mails their greetings now a—days. Get with it!"

"It gives an opportunity to touch lives with a gesture of love but a relationship is another piece of cake."

"And you are too scared!"

"When is your family coming?" I am leaving the 22nd and back the 27th."

"My kids will be here about that time. Want to do something for New Year's?'

"Sounds like a plan. In the meantime we can get together to plan our outfits and etc for the dance."

"Did you hear about Caroline's David? He had a heart attack during surgery."

"Poor Caroline, another dead partner! You would guess men would be scared of her, but I bet another one is already in the picture. I'll call you later."

Karina proceeded to take a shower and get ready for bed as she did almost every day she worked. Life was good—she thought to herself.

Police Report

Officers on patrol spotted a moped with no rear light. On approaching him, they found out the driver of the moped had outstanding warrants for probation violations, criminal attempt to manufacture methamphetamine and child support. He was staying with his brother who was notified while the moped driver got away.

Chapter 30

Two weeks to the Winter Dance at the Meadows and Karina did not have a thing to wear. She wanted an eggplant color dress, a soft flowing skirt one, maybe a peau de sois material or even chiffon. She called Barbara as soon as she got up.

"Are you game for a long day of shopping? I need a wonderful dress for the dance. I think I know exactly what I want so it should not take too long."

"Oh, yes. I need one too for me: one that isn't black nor the same one I wear every two years. Time to change."

"OK. I'll see you here in an hour. I'll drive."

Karina hung up softly, whistled her favorite tune, and the only one she knew-Yankee Doodle. She jumped in the shower for a quick refresher; and was ready to go in a jiffy. She was nervous but this time she was enjoying the feeling because it felt like she had blood in her system again.

Barbara was early and they left laughing and joking about feeling like teen agers. They went to different stores with not much luck and finally in a small unknown boutique, Karina saw the dress she had pictured getting. A halter number with a flare starting at the hips. She looked stunning in it showing her perfect long waist and small hips and hiding her stomach which had started to protrude since her move to the Meadows. The color enhanced her skin and the iridescence turned colors as she swirled around. Barbara bought a metallic blue that pleased her to tears.

Over a lunch of chicken salad and cheese bread, the two women discussed the accessories to be added to complete the ensembles.

"A successful trip, to say the least" Karina gave Barbara a big hug as they left for the car in pursuit of the accessories needed. This wasn't hard to do since the shops had such wonderful choices available.

"Mission accomplished" laughed Barbara.

The two discussed the plans all the way home making sure that Morgan felt comfortable at their reserved table. Barbara had reserved a table for eight.

The country Club at the Meadows goes all out for this dance. It is the piece of resistance of the year. It is decorated to the max with Christmas pieces from all over the world. After all, The Meadows was a mixed salad of all parts of the world and the United States. The tree was a picture of elegance and extravaganza done in gold. The tables had centerpieces of sleighs with Santa driving. The lake by the club was shining with lots of lights and boats were available for rides. The night air was chilly but the sky was clear and full of stars. It was magical.

The evening started without much fanfare while they introduced each other and relaxed in the presence of a stranger. The whole group was very formal and made small talk which turned around when Morgan explained that he had arrived from his last trip and he wanted to see Karina before returning home and make some important decisions. He expressed how impressed he was with The Meadows.

Morgan shared some funny stories about his experiences in his travels. The other couples had some trouble understanding their relationship since he was gone most of the time but was soon all dissipated. To Karina it all seemed like a distant dream where she was living a Cinderella story.

The orchestra opened the repertoire with Autumn Leaves, Karina's favorite. Morgan extended his hand and whispered: "Let's dance, gorgeous."

Morgan turned out to be a great dancer and they mambo and rumba, even a tango!. It was a great evening as she looked so graceful in Morgan's arms.

She was hoping the evening would never end as she had glimpses of dancing in her native land to the sway of palm trees except this time the sway came from her heart. She felt comfortable in Morgan's arms and accepted his kisses, short ones and long ones in her forehead, in her neck and in her hands.

Barbara wanted to go for a boat ride but Karina and Morgan decided to go home after the orchestra played its last piece, a fast conga.

On arriving, Morgan could not let go of her. The time they were waiting for and avoiding had arrived. He kissed her passionately and Karina found herself responding with desire. They soon merged into each other laying together, clinging to each other as if there was no end to it. She stretched her arms to him and he gently started kissing her as his fingers caressed her naked body discovering the different senses and how they responded to his touch. They threw themselves into discovering what their points of pleasure were without a care in the world and they both realized they fit perfectly into each others arms. A swirl of blinding desire swept them and intoxicated their senses. It was pure as well as sensual.

"This is the first time in a long time that I don't want to go home alone. You have stirred something wonderful in me." Morgan was really opening up for the first time. Karina found herself in a Zen-like state of mind. Her joy of life raised together with peace of mind. He purred like a kitten as she kissed him all over his body. She felt like an economy flier bumped to first class for no apparent reason, she turned and fell asleep in his arms.

The cold morning was more than a picker-upper. It was an antidote to the ending of a beautiful evening which pleasures kept lingering before sunrise and an experience that took Karina back to her roots. It wasn't all sensual, it touched her soul.

Morgan showed up at the kitchen all showered and Karina offered him coffee and juice. They kissed and talked about the evening laughing about the different funny things that happened like Barbara losing a shoe as she turned doing the mambo.

Morgan thanked her over and over for a memorable evening promising to stay in touch.

He left and so did Winter and Christmas and she did not hear from Morgan again. The predictable rhythm of her days became a day to day ritual trying to figure out what had happened until finally she accepted it: it was not going to work. It never did.

Police Report

A man was expressing his first amendment rights at the POA building parking lot. He crossed the line when he was laughing at and talking about POA employees as they entered the building. He was asked to leave.

Chapter 31

Spring started with a blast of yellow and orange that gets one's attention. Yellow daffodils are starting to sprout and are followed by a burst of orange tulips. From there on, the tulips start coming in all colors with their scents and trumpet blooms. The different colors can form a patchwork blanket to behold.

Karina runs around the house in a dancing mode to ward off the cool spring morning chill. Wonder and amazement were filling her days. The job at the hospital was getting easier as she learned more ways to help people. She connected with churches, charity houses and associations that were very willing to help. One of the churches had opened English as a Second Language classes (ESL) to the many newcomers. The fear of immigration and deportation was holding many of them back because they did not want to be found out. Their work did not allow them to go to school to learn the language since their hours were so undetermined and they could not chance to lose the jobs. It was a catch twenty-two.

Karina persevered in her efforts to make their lives a little easier. It made her feel useful.

Ann and Barbara were coming for lunch and a long visit that was well overdue. They arrived with wine, a cake and a pie. Karina's cooking days were pretty much over so she usually opted for something simple. Her kitchen was not the heart of her home anymore. Ordering everything was the epitome of luxury while she did her part by buttering the bread. The days when she popped out of bed like a toast from the toaster were over. Slow as a snail was her pace as she moved to make coffee and maybe some breakfast.

This afternoon she had conjured a Monte Cristo sandwich with a fruit salad and wine, tea and or coffee.

They spent the first part of the afternoon planning their adventures for the next twenty years. A German Spa to rejuvenate their tired bodies, an Italian villa to revive their very dormant sexual instincts and trips to Zermatt to ski and relax while a Frenchman massaged their feet. Belgian chocolates could be set up at the villa as they munch on croissants with lots of butter and delicious French wine. Oolala!

Barbara stopped the dreaming by asking about Daniela's trial.

"Tell me how it all went and I will not mention it again."

Karina had been reluctant to talk about it since the picture of Daniela been led out of the courtroom in shackles and orange prison garb still stirred her emotionally. Glen was sitting in the front row and so was John Miller.

"I never understood why Daniela was the only one going to prison. Glen apparently developed amnesia because he couldn't remember when Daniela came into his life and how long she had stayed. His sentence dropped from fifteen years to ten for helping the prosecution."

Karina threw her arms in the air showing frustration.

"He declared bankruptcy so he would not lose his business."

"What a creep he turned out to be! When did they bring you to the stand, Ana?" Barbara asked.

"I was brought in a couple of times. Identifying Daniela was a problem because she looks so different now. The defense really dwelt on this fact. I identified the photographs shown to me and which were displayed all over the courtroom. Pointing to Glenn as the other person was really hard on me."

"What about you, Karina?"

"Having to tell the story of the bed scene where I found Glen and Daniela was very demeaning to me."

"What an ordeal, girls!. I feel so sorry for you! A real bad experience."

"Yes, we think so too. John was charged with complicity to murder, fraud and stealing money from the insurance companies. Glen was charged with tampering with physical evidence but had to go with what the lawyers called a financial autopsy regarding his bankruptcy and Daniela with guilty of all counts facing twenty five years in prison without parole. She also had to return the money received from the insurance company. It is all very degrading to say the least. I am glad our parents are not alive to witness this disgraceful affront to our name."

The telephone interrupted the story telling . . . It was Nicolas.

"Mom, have you heard from Morgan?"

"No, Not since Christmas." Karina tried to sound collected.

"I understand that he is confined to a hospital in Minnesota."

Karina's heart did a summersault and she swallowed hard while leaning against the wall.

"Why? Do you know what happened?"

""""What his cleaning lady said when I inquired was that he went for a check up and informed her that he had to leave for a while to take care of his health, he will give her more information later."

"Nick we have to find out where he is, he has no relatives."

Ann noticed the paleness in Karina's face.

"Is everything all right? Are you ok?"

"It's ok. I'll explain in a minute." Karina answered ever so softly.

"Nick, find out what is going on and call me. Thanks"

"Girls, Morgan is in the hospital. Boy, do I have mixed feelings! On one hand I'm concerned and in the other, glad that he just didn't disappear.

Should I do something? I hope it is not that serious."

"I don't know. Wouldn't you be infringing in his privacy? There must be a reason why he did not tell you" Barbara said squeamishly.

"I'll wait and see what Nick finds out." Karina seemed determined.

They sat down to lunch and tried to lighten up the atmosphere to no avail. The conversation turned to the situation with Glen and Daniela. Both Barbara and Ann felt they are both sociopaths . . . None thought they had done anything wrong, no remorse. Karina agreed.

"He is a charmer with no sense of right nor wrong. I think he loved me as much as he will ever loved anyone but money was a bigger force. I spent many wonderful moments with him, as a matter of fact I was the happiest I have ever been and if it had not been for Daniela, I would have never found out the real Glenn. I shudder at the realization that Glen never intended to help me out with the kids and would probably had not allowed me to do it either."

"Daniela has a way to bring experiences to a peak. Looks that they were in the same page," Ann was reluctant to forgive.

"I am with you" injected Barbara as she poured more wine into the empty glasses. "Daniela deserves everything that has come to her and I hope Glenn is getting his due too."

"I'm sorry but I feel vindicated and knowing that she is put away gives me a lot of peace of mind". Ann had tears in her eyes as she expressed her feelings.

"I am so sorry that this had to happen, Ann. So very, very sorry." Karina hugged Ann and both cried some more.

"Hey we have to drop this subject, It is way too sad . . . Let's have dessert."

They grabbed their plates and moved to the living room, in front of the fire to finish a delightful afternoon although confronting in feelings.

"Coffee anyone?" Karina brought cups and the espresso to go with the desserts and proceeded to serve it. She was so grateful for such great friends and she let them know it.

Now that they had put closure on this episode of their lives, they can again enjoy the beautiful friendship that they have had. They discussed getting together again and maybe have lunch once a week. Barbara asked Ann if she played Bridge but Ann responded that she had been too busy with her life to take time out to learn. They hugged and said their good-nights and went to their respective homes.

Karina started preparing for bed when the ring of the telephone at this late an hour startled her. She rushed to answer it. It was Nicolas.

"Mom, I'm sorry to call this late but I just finished a visit with Morgan. You asked me to find out what happened, well, I did and I think you should know. I wanted to catch you now since our days are so hectic."

"Oh, Nick, I thought something was wrong!. Tell me, I'm all ears"

Karina was somewhat sarcastic.

"After a wonderful time spent with you, he came home thinking of quitting his job and spending more time getting to know you. He had a pain in his groin and on examining it, he felt a lump on his right testicle. When two days later, it had not gone away, he went for tests and was found with testicular cancer, the Seminoma kind. He did not want to put you through the ordeal that this could be, so he decided it was better to wait and find out what was in store for him. After a long discussion with the doctors, he opted for surgery and moved to Minnesota to be near the hospital where he would undergo an intensive therapy. He was on stage one which is limited to the testis."

"And it did not occur to him that maybe I needed to know that?

Karina interrupted.

"According to him, he thought it best to leave you with the good memory of your last time together. Mom, he had found out he had cancer, be real!"

"So, where is he, Is he all right? What are his plans?"

"There is risk of bleeding and infection and he has to be near his doctor. He will need treatments every three months but apparently all has been removed. He will need radiation but the doctor has promised recovery. He did not want to put you on this spot. Now that he knows he will be all right, he wanted to discuss the ordeal with you and apologize for not communicating. I think you should at least give him one break."

"I have to digest all of it. Thank you sweetheart for all your concern. I love you. I'll sleep on it."

Karina, again had mixed feelings, she went to bed with a smirk on her face.

Chapter 32

Karina had survived the terrible Summer heat that seemed to linger on. The Meadows had not experienced such Summer but the whole world was on strike. There was a feeling of endings in the air as if we were facing a disaster or a big change. Karina was all for change so she hoped for that, a good change though.

She had started preparing for a visit from Adriana and the kids. It was so uncomfortably hot and she did not know where she would take them other than the make believe beach near her home or the swimming pool. It was miserable outside for the children to play so she must plan inside activities. She planned as she walked around getting ready to go to work.

The outpouring of out-of-wedlock babies was becoming a social catastrophe. We know that the breakdown of the family unit is bad for the children.

Social capital is denied to these children who are born and/or raised in single-parents homes. Karina blamed it all on the fall of our value system. These partnerships are not geared to stay together and we face a disoriented group of adults or young people. Karina felt that we encourage these births and these values by supporting them financially. The Hispanic population is following the trend. Their united but not scrambled relationships are causing more pain and problems in our culture than the stability they are looking for.

She thought about Morgan on her drive into town. He was the first man she had considered for a relationship since Glenn. She wondered if she was just attracted to the impossibility present. She was somewhat apprehensive. This man who possesses such an alarming vitality had no awareness of how much she liked him or maybe acceptance is a better word. She felt unsettled, frustrated but she had to put these feelings aside and concentrate on the reality of her life. She has to listen to Morgan, she doesn't have to believe him, after all he is a sick man.

Arriving at her job, a doctor was already waiting for her.

"Elena's PAP smear was positive and we need to do further testing which will include a biopsy."

Karina explained the situation to a very scared Elena who burst into tears without understanding the full implication of the diagnosis. She wanted this baby and that was all she cared about. Karina did her best to calm her down and she was scheduled for a biopsy.

Karina opened the door to the next patient's room to face a bewildered nurse practitioner. Mrs. Rivera, a forty two years old lady explains to Karina that she separated from her husband and decided to move to a new apartment. Freddy, a friend of her husband's came to help her out and "one thing led to another and here I am pregnant".

"Well you are considered a risk because of your age, I want you to know that. Is Freddy going to be part of this experience?"

A very redundant no came out of her mouth: another sad truth that these women had to face.

This was our clientele at its best. Certainly not mellow nor inspiring, crudeness and merciless was their survival and all they knew. Ignorance was their self-defense.

The sonographer called Karina to look at a sonogram of a baby who was growing without a brain. This baby was Emilia's first born. We advised her to terminate the pregnancy but she refused claiming that she would leave it to God and she would wait for a miracle.

(The pregnancy progressed to the full term and Emilia gave birth to a baby without a brain who lasted a couple of hours, long enough to be baptized and for Emilia to hold him in her arms)

Such moments of revelations are common in the clinic. Karina felt impotent and this frustrated her. She felt helping them financially broke down their dignity and ambition. She had to remind herself that she was just an echo. A stark contrast to the nurses and doctors even the director who did not have the opportunity to see" the other side of the coin."

These revelations often happened when one least expected and not easy to deal with. It was still gratifying because Karina felt she was helping even if the others didn't think so.

Again, Morgan inspired her because he gave so freely although maybe this is where he went to achieve immortality. She wondered if she would see him again.

She drove quietly home as she planned mentally her trip with her Singles' group. They were attending a week-end trip to one of the mountain resorts. She reluctantly had joined this club hoping she would stay busy and so able to get Morgan out of her mind. She packed lightly and went to bed. She was really tired.

Gloria picked her up early Saturday morning. The trip in itself was very scenic and enjoyable. They stopped at a local restaurant for lunch and bought some home-made pies for dinner. The cabin was cozy and close to all attractions except restaurants. It was a good thing that they had brought food. They picked the rooms they were to occupy and went for a walk. Dinner was already on the table when they returned. Everyone was delighted about the pies. They set up a couple of tables for Bridge and they joked and laughed the night away.

In the morning, one of the members, who apparently was dating the president, wanted to trade his room with the girl that was rooming with Janet so he could sleep with his beloved. Bill offered Marian two hundred dollars for the trade which Marian gladly did and they proceeded to trade rooms. Karina was shocked and disgusted. She felt they should have kept their rendezvous private, when they were alone. Next morning Karina left the cabin with Barbara who felt like she did.

"I know what you are going to say."

Barbara tried to beat Karina to the complaining.

"This is the way it is. It is happening everywhere."

"Maybe, but I don't need to be part of it. This is so insulting, humiliating. Bargaining for sex is what is. I find it disgusting".

Karina started crying. Just when she thought she was starting to belong.

"I'm sorry Barbara, I think I am going to move near my kids and see my grandchildren grow up before I die."

"I know how you feel but don't make any decisions while this episode is vivid in your mind. I have accepted all the going-ons because I have to stay. I don't have the option of living near my kids. They really don't want me near."

"I promise I'll do that. I don't believe that your kids don't want you, maybe not living with them but definitely near."

They said nothing more. Barbara knew Karina well enough to know that she needed time to sort it all out. She had gone through a lot in a very short time. They stopped in front of Karina's place and Barbara promised to call her tomorrow. Karina went in in silence. She pushed the message button on her machine and surprisingly there was another call from Morgan.

"I need to talk to you. I have a lot of explaining to do". Morgan sounded very apologetic.

Karina pushed erase and went to bed. She was not ready and was very afraid of getting hurt again.

It was a calm October afternoon. Summer was coming to an end which made Karina very happy. Gone were the 97 degree temperatures and in were the nice cool breezes of Autumn. Karina kept pushing the erase button on Morgan's calls. She felt tempted many times to answer but now that she knew he was fine, she did not want to go there again.

She had just finished cleaning house and packing those accumulated extras that we keep over the years, she decided to take a break and have a cup of tea. She put her legs on the hassock and laid her head on the back of the couch and s-t-r-e-t-c-h-e-d. She chanted a long OHM and took a sip of tea when the door bell tensed her up again. She debated against answering but someone was very persistent. She got up and opened the door and to her amazement, there stood non other than Dr. Davies.

"May I come in?"

Karina responded by moving her arm in a please do gesture. She was speechless.

Morgan walked in and followed her steps into the living room.

"Please listen to me even if it is only to find forgiveness. I missed you and you have inspired me enough to want to form another relationship. Can we start where we left off? A new bridge to cross? Now that I know that I'll be healthy I dare ask you to let me hold your hand the rest of our way."

"Is this offer opened for negotiations?" Karina surprised herself with her answer.

Morgan took her in his arms and kissed her over and over . . . .

Autumn was here again and the weather was more to her liking. She always liked the fall weather and the color change. Pretty soon she would get ready for her visit with the children and all would go back to normal. She sat down with a cup of coffee and looked out as the leaves started to get yellow and red. There was the smell of freshness all around and she felt relaxed.

There was a lot for her to think about and she was opened to cross the bridge in front of her no matter how short it would turn out to be.